A Boy from Ireland

A Boy from Ireland

A Novel by

Marie Raphael

A Karen and Michael Braziller Book

PERSEA BOOKS/NEW YORK

Persea Books
277 Broadway, Suite 708
New York, NY 10007

Library-in-Congress Cataloging-in-Publication Data
Raphael, Marie.
A Boy from Ireland : a novel / Marie Raphael. — 1st ed.
    p. cm.
"A Karen and Michael Braziller book."
Summary: Bullied because of the English father he barely remembers, four-teen-year-old Liam gladly leaves Connemara, Ireland, in 1901 with his uncle and sister, but his problems follow them to Hell's Kitchen in New York City, until he finds a way to leave the past behind.
    ISBN 978-0-89255-426-3 (hardcover : alk. paper)
    [1. Emigration and immigration—Fiction. 2. Immigrants—New York (State)—New York—Fiction. 3. Irish Americans—Fiction. 4. Prejudices—Fiction. 5. Family—Fiction. 6. Horses—Fiction. 7. New York (N.Y.)—History—1898–1951— Fiction. 8. Ireland—History—1837-1901—Fiction.] I. Title.
PZ7.R18122Boy 2007
[Fic]—dc22
                                    2007005147

Designed by Rita Lascaro. Typeset in Cochin.
Printed on recycled, acid-free paper.
Manufactured in the United States of America.

First trade paperback and electronic book editions, 2014

To my sons, Nick and Neil,
love always

A Boy from Ireland

CHAPTER ONE

NOT FAR FROM LIAM, five boys stood in the shadow of an oak tree, whose long, bare branches poked out like spikes. The boys were older than Liam, and they examined him coldly, as if he were an enemy. But Liam recognized only one, the tallest. Just this morning, before Sunday Mass began in St. Joseph's church, that boy had turned in Liam's direction, lips closing in a disapproving line.

Now, nodding at Liam, he said something to the other boys, who laughed. They were laughing at him, Liam knew. Angrily, he turned his back on them.

A hundred yards ahead of him, where two roads crossed, a fiddler stood in a patch of thin March sunlight and tuned his strings. Dancers were taking their places. Beyond them, Liam's older sister and another girl sat on a stone wall, talking.

If the girls here talked to Alice Ann, the boys didn't, and not one had asked her to dance. The boys treated her the way they were treating him, like an unwanted stranger. And he and Alice Ann were strangers. After Mum died, they had been sent here—to Connemara and to Uncle Patrick, her brother. They had arrived only five days ago, after crossing from Ireland's eastern shore to its western shore on a train that rocked back and forth, as if it wanted to jump the tracks and go its own way.

Thinking of that journey, Liam stripped the bark from a stick that was almost as long as his arm. With a knife he had taken from Uncle Patrick's table that morning, he sharpened its end into a point. A minute passed, and then another. Suddenly, just as chaffinches exploded out of a bush in front of Liam, a hand clamped down on his mouth. The knife was ripped from his hand. He had been standing at the very edge of a steep incline, and in a single moment four boys pulled him down it and out of sight. They gripped his arms and waist, lifting him halfway off the ground, and carried him through the brush. Behind three towering rocks, they threw him to the ground.

"We have him, Michael," one of them announced.

The boy named Michael, the tall boy who had been at church, looked down at Liam and grinned. "Quick work you made of it, and no one is the wiser."

The boy who pinned down Liam's shoulders said, "Didn't someone tell us he's fourteen? The runt of the lit- ter, that is what he is then." He studied Liam and added, "He's like a ghost with those pale blue eyes of his."

"They are English eyes. That's all they are," another boy replied. He had freckled cheeks. The freckles were the same color as the ginger-colored hair that spilled over his high forehead.

"Give the knife over, Colin," the boy named Michael said to him.

At the order, Colin handed Michael the knife he had taken from Liam. "Aye, aye, Commandant," he said. "Let us take care of this little Englishman." His ears stuck out. They were freckled, too.

Michael crouched beside Liam, yanking off his cap. "The hair on your skull, 'tis English hair, fine, wavy English hair." He leaned forward and tapped the knife's blade on Liam's throat. Swallowing, Liam felt its tip ride along his Adam's apple. "And English blood runs in these veins of yours. In this part of Ireland we are not fond of the English. Do you know why that is, Liam Tanner?" In the dusky light, Michael's gray eyes were almost black. He leaned closer. "Tanner. 'Tis a rotten English name."

He spoke in Gaelic, the Irish tongue. All the boys did. Liam wanted to tell them that his mother had spoken Gaelic with him and Alice Ann when they were small, so they would learn it. Like them, she had grown up in Connemara. She was Irish like they were. He was Irish, too—half-Irish.

And he was English, like his father. What the boys said was true.

Michael spoke again, spitting the words out. "In famine times, who was it that turned my grandfather out and burned his cabin down so he would not come back, not ever again?"

When Liam didn't answer, he said more sharply, "Who was it? And who took Ireland's land, making tenants of us all—my grandfather and his grandfather and everyone else?"

They hated the English and wanted him to denounce his father. Liam closed his fingers into a fist, swearing he wouldn't.

The knife trailed across his throat. "Who was it forbade the Irish tongue and forced a foreign tongue upon us?" Michael asked.

"That was long ago, a century ago and more. It does not happen now," Liam argued. Fright caught the words up in his throat.

"My father talks of it, my grandmother does, of how the English punished us if we spoke Gaelic. They were Protestant, and they chased the Catholic bishops out of Ireland. They branded the priests who resisted. Long ago or not, we won't forgive that, not ever." The knife traveled to Liam's forehead. Held there, its tip pricked his skin. "Who branded the priests? Tell us. Is that not a fine tale?"

A snipe flew out of the brush with a cry. A trace of white flashed at the edge of its wings.

"Who? Say it!" Michael hissed. The knife pressed harder.

They would brand him. That is why they had caught him—to cut his forehead to the bone and carve their mark.

"'Tis always the same answer—the English, like you!" Michael declared.

Liam felt a trickle of blood run down his temple. He felt his heart beating. He might be running, it pumped so hard. Michael grabbed his hair and yanked it violently. The blade came down. With all his might Liam tried to dodge, twisting away. Then Michael was hacking his hair off, not branding him. Michael was saying, "Fight me like that and I will scalp you. See if I don't! Be still!"

After they let him rise, Michael held the knife up. "Your uncle will want this back. Tell him Michael Lanigan returned it. Sure your uncle can understand what we did. Everyone has heard Patrick Cavanaugh talk of how his sister went off with that father of yours to breed English brats."

Michael Lanigan threw the knife at Liam blade first, so that he could not grab it. It fell at his feet. When he bent to pick it up, the tall, ginger-haired boy named Colin jeered, "He is a fine sight. His head is as bare as a babe's bottom."

Another boy laughed. Liam felt a stinging in his eyes. He gripped the knife's handle as hard as he could, straightening. He had not cried since he was a child, except at Mum's dying.

He would not cry now. He stared evenly at a boy whose arms were folded across his thick chest and at another who tugged absentmindedly at his ear, as if nothing at all were happening.

"You may go. We are done for now," Michael said finally. He was taller than any of the others, the shadow of a beard on his cheeks.

Colin grinned at Liam. "If you would care to join us

again, Liam Tanner, you are always welcome. Sure you know that."

Liam passed out of the circle, expecting the boys to grab him at the last moment. They didn't. They let him go. He walked through the deep brush.

When he reached the road, Liam saw a pony that was tethered to an elderberry bush with an old rope. In that moment he had a sharp memory. Earlier in the day Michael Lanigan had stood beside this animal. Liam had hardly looked at Michael then. He had examined this mare instead, certain that she was one of the Connemara ponies his mother had described. Their Irish blood was mixed with blood from Arabian horses that swam ashore centuries ago, when ships in the Spanish Armada had gone down in a great storm off Ireland's western coast. Arabian blood gave the ponies their height, but they were Irish from head to hoof, Mum had said. Like the Irish, they lived on little and flourished all the same. They could gallop across rough terrain that would bring down Lord Clapham's fine, long-legged thoroughbreds.

That was what he had thought before. Now what Liam thought was that the pony was Michael's. As if she were his own, he walked straight up to her and jerked her reins free. The pony startled. Clutching at her neck for purchase, Liam vaulted onto her bare back.

There was a shout. When Michael ran forward, Liam jabbed the pony with his heels and headed straight at him. Riding the mare, he towered over Michael. Suddenly he was the powerful one, and Michael was the fearful one. At the last moment, Michael threw himself out of the way.

When Liam looked back, he saw Michael writhing on the ground in pain, holding onto his knee, and he saw Alice Ann. She ran into the road, dark hair flying, her blue skirt swaying. She raised her arms, as if she were pleading with him to come back.

But his sister didn't know that the boys had attacked him. They'd won then, but now, with Michael's own horse under him, he was winning, and he couldn't go back. Ahead, sunlight was streaming across the sloping fields, as if it were being spilled from a giant pitcher by some reckless god up in the sky. It splattered everywhere. Liam whooped and urged the pony into a gallop. He looked straight between the pony's ears. The way ahead was clear. To keep his seat he tucked his heels in, clamping tightly.

He rode the pony until she was slick with sweat. Even then, she jumped forward when Liam tapped his heels against her flanks and clucked into her ear. In spite of her ragged forelock and her tattered rope halter, she reminded Liam of a racehorse Lord Clapham owned, an odd-looking piebald stallion, Morengo, named after the horse Napoleon rode. It was the eager way the pony's head nosed forward as they raced along the road. Pressed close to her neck, her mane whipping about him, Liam felt half-horse himself.

A half-mile from his uncle's field, Liam slowed the pony to a walk. Once in the field, he led her in wide circles around a pine stump to cool her down. When she was no longer breathing hard, Liam halted.

He pulled off his shirt and used it to rub the pony's coat from rump to shoulder. When she gave a snort, Liam said, "I would as soon hear your snorting as any human talk." He stroked her nose. "All my life I've been with horses. Father carried me on one when I was four days old, they tell me, and I could ride all by myself when I was three. Lord Clapham had a fine stable. He had hunters and carriage horses and horses the ladies rode. I shined the hooves of Lady Clapham's pretty mare until they were as bright as the silver plate Mum polished every Saturday morning up in the great house. There were race horses, too, a half-dozen of them."

Liam had ridden those fast horses. He had even ridden Morengo, Lord Clapham's favorite racehorse, a horse he let few people near, a horse that would do anything Liam asked. The boys in the woods had mocked him for being small, but that meant he was light on a horse's back. He had a jockey's wiry build and weighed what a jockey should, and because of that, Lord Clapham's trainer had favored him. When he wanted to give a horse a real ride, Mr. Laurent would pass right by the other exercise boys and call out, "You, Liam, hop to it! Mount up!"

Liam would. He had loved the cold rush of morning wind that the animal created, thundering along a hard track. In those minutes he flew into another world. There was nothing but the horse that drove forward under him. There were no humans. There were no boys who wanted to trap him.

He scratched between the pony's ears and said, "It's

the horses I miss more than anything. You understand that, don't you?" When the pony tossed her head, Liam said, "I've no oats for you, no corn, but there's water."

He led the pony down the cliff trail, which crossed a stream. There he halted so she could drink. Once she raised her head and glanced at the inlet below them, where small waves wrinkled the water's surface. Wings outstretched, two cormorants flew past. "Mum fished on that water," he told the mare. "She'd go out with her father in a little boat he had, and they'd bring home dabs and turbot for her own mum to cook. They'd bait the hooks with mayflies."

Ears tilting forward, the pony seemed to be listening to every word he said. Some claimed that horses could understand human speech, and Liam thought they might. Some even insisted that before Noah's flood, horses had talked. Liam sometimes believed they tried to. The pony seemed to be trying to say something now, her tail swishing back and forth and back and forth.

"Mum talked of Connemara all the time. There were chieftains here once and grand, brave warriors."

A warrior—if he were a warrior, he would take revenge for what the older boys had done.

The pony beside him, Liam climbed up the trail. There was the clip-clop of her hooves and the clip-clop of his thoughts as he recalled all that had happened to him in the woods. Angrily, he ran a hand across the uneven bristles of hair on his head.

Even before he reached the cliff's crest, Liam had

thought of a way he could strike back at the boys. He tugged at the pony's reins to hurry her across the field.

At the pine stump he picked up the knife he had left there. He thought he heard the distant, low hooting of an owl but wasn't certain what the sound was. He wasn't certain if he could do what he had just told himself he would do to the pony either. Then he remembered how he had wiped fresh blood from his scalp when he emerged from the woods.

Quickly, before he could hesitate again, he slashed at the mare's tousled forelock with his uncle's knife. As if she were posing a question of some kind, the mare rolled her eyes back.

Liam next moved to her side and cut at her mane. In a dozen hard strokes it was all but gone. Uneasy, the pony stepped forward. He slipped his arms around her craned neck. "Stay put now. I won't hurt you," he said. She nickered, answering, the way horses would always answer him.

Slowly he slipped along the pony's side, stroking her. She stayed in place while Liam sawed the hair from her tail.

Done, he mounted and pressed her into a trot. There had been a mane before that flew backwards as they raced. Now there was only stubble. They passed a woman with a huge basket lashed to her back. She skittered out of their way, waving Liam on. Past Clifden, Liam spied the big pointed rock that marked the Lanigan's holdings, which his uncle had pointed out five days ago, the day he and Alice Ann had arrived. Their belongings at their feet, they were riding in the cart Uncle Patrick had borrowed, which was pulled by a borrowed donkey. "Over there," Uncle Patrick had barked, stabbing his finger into the air, "neighbors of ours live over there—the Lanigans. This is their land."

Liam halted the pony by the rock and dismounted. With her mane and forelock gone, she looked foolish. Her tail was like a short stick. Liam gently slapped her on the rump. "Go now," he said. "Go home."

The pony tossed her head and moved off. At the sight of her, Michael would read the message he was delivering. He would know it for a battle cry.

Fear stirred inside Liam the way it had when, in the woods, Michael's face had loomed over his, the nose large, the eyes almost black. He pushed the feeling back. The boys had stripped his hair off his head, and now he was retaliating because he had to.

CHAPTER TWO

The next morning, Uncle Patrick said to Liam, "Never are you to take anything of mine, not a knife, not anything!" He plucked a black leather strap from a nail on the wall. "Bend over, boyo. Your hands on the table! Go on. Do what you're told!"

Eyes shut, clutching the table, Liam waited for a long and hated moment before he heard the hiss of leather and felt the first jolt of pain. The next stroke came. Liam drew breath between clenched teeth. In all, there were a half-dozen hard lashes. When it was over, Liam took a deep breath, trying to stop the trembling in his hands. He turned to face his uncle, who was too tall and too close. Liam wanted to step back, away from him, but he made his feet stay where they were. His uncle's hand reached forward. He swept the cap off Liam's head. In spite of himself, Liam flinched.

"Who did that to you?" Uncle Patrick ran his fingers across the stubble of hair on Liam's head.

"Boys," Liam answered.

"What boys?"

"I didn't know them."

"And the why of it? Did you not know that either?"

"No, Uncle," Liam lied. He would not tell Uncle Patrick that the boys had attacked him for his English blood. He knew that his uncle hated the English as much as the boys did.

They ate breakfast in silence, with Uncle Patrick frowning into his bowl and Alice Ann throwing Liam worried looks.

When they were done with breakfast, Liam and his uncle walked out to the field. Liam shivered in the cold March wind. A thick fog swallowed up the land around them. After two hours, it rose like a curtain on a stage, so that Liam could see the world that surrounded them. The landscape was shot through with sun. The uneven ground descended to a cliff. He could picture his mother as a child, racing barefoot toward it, her dark hair tumbling over her small shoulders. She had once said that when she was little, she had never walked if she could run. Beyond the cliff was an immense, glittering ocean.

His mother had been a child in this place, and so had her brother. It was impossible to imagine Uncle Patrick as a child though. At Liam's side, bent over, his shoulders made sharp points. His chest was narrow. Black suspenders kept his pants from slipping over equally narrow hips. Uncle Patrick worked silently, using a long stick to bore a hole in a ridge that was made of seaweed and manure and crushed shell. He shoved a thick wedge of potato into the hole. In weeks, a plant would sprout from it. Dozens of these seed potatoes were set out along the ridge. Never looking up, Uncle Patrick moved from one to the next.

Liam picked up another rock and threw it into the basket at his feet. He would flee from this uncle if he could.

They were returning to the cabin for their mid-day meal when Liam saw a postman pedaling toward them. A white mailbag was tied to a carrier at the front of his large bicycle. When he reached them, the postman held up a letter and grinned. "For a Mister Patrick Cavanaugh," he announced to Liam's uncle. "This is a letter you'll be wanting. It is from one of the female persuasion or so it appears." He winked and grinned. "A fine hand she has."

"Give it over, Kevin Mahoney, and no need do I have of idle remarks about the post," Uncle Patrick growled.

The postman rode off, skirting three huge potholes. Uncle Patrick peered at his letter while Liam wondered what woman would ever want to write to his uncle.

Inside the cabin, Alice Ann was setting a jug of buttermilk on the small, battered table. Her head was bent, and dark hair tumbled across her face, screening it from view. The sleeves of her dress were pushed up to the elbows, and made her long arms seem longer yet. Uncle Patrick propped the letter against the jug. "I'll wash," he said to her. "I need the basin and water."

Alice Ann straightened and swept the hair back from her face with two hands, latching the thick tresses behind her ears. She had brown eyes. Thick, arching brows almost met in the space above her nose. She was older than Liam by two years and taller by two or three inches and turning from a girl into a woman. Liam thought of how she used to giggle like a girl when she was telling a story about someone foolish, like Lady Clapham's niece, who came on visits from Dublin and who would sometimes shriek at nothing, at mouse droppings she spied or a circling bee.

That was in Kildare. But now, facing Uncle Patrick, Alice Ann wore a serious expression. She was nodding obediently. "Yes, Uncle," she said.

Uncle Patrick peered at her closely, as if he were trying to remember just who she was, while Alice Ann smoothed her thin woolen skirt. She did that when she was lost in thought, the way Mum used to do. Then she picked up a basin and opened the cabin door. Outside, from a rain barrel, she scooped up water with a tin can and splashed it into the basin. When she returned, Uncle Patrick's great sow was right behind her. The sow was round as a barrel, her oatmeal-colored skin splattered with mud. She snuffled at Alice Ann's legs. Alice Ann stamped her foot to drive the beast back. "Shoo! Go!" she yelped and shut the door with a single swing of her hip. The pig's great snout was visible in the gap under the wooden doorframe.

"Brood after brood of piglets she produces, that sow," Uncle Patrick grumbled. "Earns her keep in this house, she does. As much a right she has here as the two of you. That must be said." He wet his hands in the basin that

Alice Ann set down and rubbed at them with a bar of brown soap.

While Liam washed in his turn, Alice Ann busied herself at the hearth. She ladled soup into two tin plates with high sides and into a wooden bowl. The bowl was set in front of Uncle Patrick, a tin plate in front of Liam. In the broth were potatoes, cabbage, turnips, and onions, and the wild watercress and sorrel Alice Ann had collected for seasoning. Alice Ann took the other tin plate for herself and sat down beside them.

At Lord Clapham's, at a kitchen table six times the size of this one, the head butler had led a score of servants in grace, his voice thundering. Everyone had repeated the prayer after him. Now Uncle Patrick closed his eyes to pray and his lips moved, but the words were inaudible.

Done with his silent prayer, Uncle Patrick took three mouthfuls of soup before turning abruptly on Liam. "You, boyo," he said, "this letter." He grabbed the square envelope from its place and held it up. "They are not Irish stamps. You can see that much, can you not?"

"I can, Uncle."

"Where are they from then?"

"England?" Alice Ann asked.

"It was not you I was speaking to, missy, but you take note. I'll say this the once only. No need have we of letters from England. In this great country of Ireland, we have no need of the English at all—not their lawn tennis or their Queen Victoria, not their blooming language." He glared at the jug of buttermilk, as if it were an enemy.

"That stamp you see, it is a stamp from the United States," he said, "and the man pictured on it is their Benjamin Franklin. He fought for his country's independence from Britain—the same as Ireland has through all these centuries. Resist we will until her hold is broken entirely. I will tell you that."

Liam could see the drops of soup on Uncle Patrick's mustache when he turned, trapping Liam in his stern stare. The mustache was skimpy and thin, like all the rest of him. "Your Mum told me she begged Lord Clapham to let you have some schooling. But what word was ever uttered in that school of yours, there in Kildare, of England's robbing Ireland's lands—when Henry the Eighth came to the throne those three hundred and fifty years ago, when their Queen Elizabeth ruled after him?"

It was true, Liam admitted to himself. The schoolmaster, Mr. Sterling, was English and never mentioned England's wrongdoings. Mr. Sterling had a triple chin that wobbled when he hollered at his pupils. Before dismissing them from lessons, he would make the boys face a portrait of England's Queen Victoria and shout, "God save the Queen," three times in a row.

Uncle Patrick passed a finger across his dry lips. He said, "What did you learn, off in Kildare, about the famines or anything else?"

"Mum talked about the famines," Liam answered. "When grandfather was a young man, he came out of his father's cabin and saw that the potato plants had turned black from blight in a single night. He knelt in the field and prayed, afraid they all might starve. Mum said people would walk among the dead plants, moaning and crying."

Uncle Patrick's hands were always moving. Now he scratched slowly at his nose. A line of dirt ran under each of his fingernails in spite of the washing-up. Liam looked at the line just like it under his own nails, and he said, "In Clifden, there was a workhouse for people who were starving. They laid the tracks for the railroad. Some died because they were too weak to do the work. Mum told us everything."

"That mother of yours—was it not your mother who went off to Lord Clapham's grand estate? Off she went with your father to serve an English lord."

Alice Ann interrupted. "The letter is from the United States. Who wrote you from there, Uncle?" His older sister interrupted, Liam knew, to draw his uncle's attention away and protect him.

He could protect himself. "They did nothing wrong, not my mother, not my father either," he said into his uncle's face.

"A mongrel they made of you," Uncle Patrick replied. "But I'll correct that if I can. You'll work beside me, scraping and scratching at rocks like I've done all my life, until the Irish blood rises up in your veins."

Angrily, he stood and stomped off, the letter in his hand. Liam still did not know who had written it.

Late that night, Liam lay down in a corner of the cabin and wrapped himself in his blanket. He could smell peat smoke from the fireplace. The earthen floor beneath him was hard. From a rolled-up handkerchief he took out the blue-gray stone he kept there, a stone he had taken from the ground beside Mum's grave. He clasped it in his hand while he listened to Uncle Patrick's steady snoring.

When he heard a rustling noise, Liam turned his head. It was Alice Ann, who crept toward him. When she reached him, she whispered, "Why did the boys attack you? Why did they do it?"

"Because Father was English. That's why."

"That makes no sense, Liam, none at all." Cold, she rubbed at her arms. "But it's why Uncle Patrick is hard on you, too. Because Mum married Father, an Englishman."

Liam knew the story. Their father had been Lord Clapham's head groom. He had traveled from Lord Clapham's estate in the east to Lord Clapham's holdings in Connemara on some business concerning the breeding of horses. Here, he met their mother. Seven months later, they married.

"You and Father were as alike as two peas in a pod, Mum always said," Alice Ann murmured.

Liam knew he had his father's blue eyes. More than once Mum had told him that he had his father's high forehead, straight eyebrows, high cheekbones, and pointed chin, too. He had his curling, dark blond hair.

Alice Ann said, "Uncle Patrick looks at you and he sees Father. He's angry at Father, if truth be told, not you."

His sister looked nothing at all like their father, not from the moment she was born, Mum used to say. They named her Alice Ann after Father's own mother, so she would have something of Father's, a name if nothing else.

"Here, no one sees us for who we are," he said. "They look at us and they see Father or Lord Clapham. They see hated ghosts."

"Ghosts—you're right, they see ghosts, not us." He could barely make out the words Alice Ann whispered. "If only it was like it was before," she added. "I wish we could have the past back. I wish I could wake up tomorrow in Kildare."

The past—it was Mum alive. It was Fiona, a girl he fancied, who had cried the morning he left. It was the stable at night and the muffled breathing of the horses when he went there before bed.

But in Kildare there was also Lord Clapham's son-in-law, who would bellow at the stable boys as if they were half-wits. "In Kildare, we were Irish, you and Mum and myself," Liam said. "And we never had much. The English rule Ireland. They intend to keep what they've taken. Uncle Patrick is right about that."

At the mention of his name, their uncle stirred in his sleep. Alice Ann put a finger to her lips, but Liam finished his thought in a quiet voice. "There, we were Irish and kept down. And here, we are English and hated for it."

"Not everyone hates us. At the dance there was a woman who makes lace, and she said she would teach me how. And the girls were kind to me."

"But the boys wouldn't speak to you. They wouldn't dance with you."

"No," Alice Ann agreed.

"You'll never dance again if you stay here, I tell you."

From the opposite side of the room, Uncle Patrick muttered in his sleep. Afraid he was waking, Alice Ann scurried away.

Alone, Liam asked himself the questions he had wanted to ask her. How could they escape, and if they did, where could they go? They were Irish and they were English, both, and they belonged nowhere at all.

"The call has been issued, then," the strange man with the large mustache was saying as Liam came into the cabin the next morning. He set the eggs he had collected next to the crock where butter was kept.

The man was a giant. Back straight, he sat on a short, three-legged stool that seemed like it might break under his weight. Under the stool was a dog, a brown and white terrier. He rose and crossed the floor. Nostrils quivering with interest, he sniffed at Liam's legs, but the stranger didn't seem to notice Liam at all. The stranger held Uncle Patrick's letter in his hands. "We will answer the call, surely," he said in an excited voice.

"Aye, answer it we will. The people there have not forgotten Ireland's plight," Uncle Patrick replied. "They have given before. They will give again." He picked up a fishing net that lay on the table and began mending the holes in it, complaining of the dogfish that had made them. From the rafter over his head, on a line made of tight twists of straw, hung small smoked fish that had been caught in that net months before.

Tying broken filaments in the netting, Uncle Patrick was silent. So was the stranger, who teased strands from a plug of tobacco and tapped them into a long-stemmed clay pipe. Liam wanted to shout at them to talk.

Finally Uncle Patrick did. "Thousands fill the streets come Saint Patrick's Day. That is what Tess McCathery writes in her letter. The Irish there do not forget Ireland."

Smoke drifted from the stranger's mouth when he spoke. "A grand opportunity this is. New York offers us an opportunity!"

"New York?" Liam burst out. "Are you going to New York City?"

Uncle Patrick stared at him. "Bent on interrupting us, he is, this one. He is much in need of manners."

"Patrick, come, come." The stranger's pipe had burned out. He knocked the ashes onto the dirt floor. "Why it does no harm to give the lad the information he is seeking." He turned toward Liam, smiling. The creases set into the corners of his mouth and the corners of his brown eyes were made from smiling. "Aye, New York City itself, that is where we are going. We will leave soon enough, in a fortnight."

Uncle Patrick said, "I must take that boy there and his sister." The light that came through the door stopped just short of where he sat, leaving him in shadows. "Didn't I promise my sister Molly that I'd not desert them? I'll keep my word." He pointed at Liam. "And before I'm done with this one, he will know what it means to be Irish."

The stranger drummed his fingers on the table for a moment, glancing at Liam. "He will have company, your nephew will," he said. "My oldest boy will be coming. Sure it is time he had a taste of the business, long past time. We can set him to the task, even if it is only passing the hat after a talk we give or putting up notices to announce it."

Lost in his own thoughts, Liam hardly heard what the stranger said. In fourteen days they would leave here. They would cross an ocean. His heart leapt.

Seeing Liam's glad look, Uncle Patrick grumbled, "'Tis not a holiday, boyo. You will find work there, you and your sister, the both of you. In New York you'll earn your keep. Mark what I say." His eyes narrowed. "You know enough about our business then, and we have things to talk about here that are no concern of yours."

Dismissed, Liam went outside. Twenty minutes later, the stranger emerged from the cabin, the terrier at his heels. When the dog noticed Uncle Patrick's orange cat, which was basking in the sun by the gate, he lit out after her. The cat ran for her life, straight into the brambles.

Liam was glad. He hated the cat, which was kept on the place to kill mice and rats. The first time they'd met, he had tried to pet her and she had clawed at his hand.

In fourteen days, he would be rid of that spitting, wild-eyed creature forever.

CHAPTER THREE

SUNDAY CAME AROUND AGAIN. Liam and Alice Ann and their uncle left the cabin for church. On the road, their uncle drew ahead of them. His walk was slightly unbalanced, as if one leg were shorter than the other.

"You are sure it is New York?" Alice Ann asked.

"I'm positive," Liam answered.

"It is the republican cause surely, if they were talking of raising funds—an independent Irish republic, Ireland for the Irish and no union with England, not now and not ever," Alice Ann said. "The Fenians wanted that, and the Irish Republican Brotherhood did, too. Men go to America to find money to fight for that still. Uncle will be one of them then."

"I don't care why we are going. All that matters is that we are," Liam said. "We're going to America!"

"But in the end we will return, and we'll be eating uncle's cabbages and potatoes once again." Alice Ann looked down, watching her polished shoes, making sure they stayed out of the wet mud. She didn't see the rabbit that darted into view. Liam noticed how it skittered from right to left to confuse any hawk or fox that might be hunting, and he remembered how his father had liked to hunt rabbits. Sometimes his father would take him along, pushing the undergrowth aside for him in the woods. He had trailed so closely behind his father that he could have been his father's third leg.

Then, without warning, his father had gone away.

Liam took a breath of the salty air. He said to Alice Ann, "Why would Mum never talk about Father and what happened? Why wouldn't she say where he went?"

"Lord Clapham made him go. That's all I know." Alice Ann looked out to the sea. "A wagon came, and he put his things into it, and he was shouting at Mum. I remember all that. I remember running alongside the wagon when he left. He didn't look up. He kept his head buried in his hands. He never looked at me."

She had told him this before. Together, they had always sifted through the memories they kept of their father, trading them back and forth, like children traded marbles. Alice Ann stumbled on a stone. She caught herself.

"Haven't we heard that the Irish go to New York City by the thousands?" Liam asked her. "We might find him there."

There was something bitter in his older sister's tone when she said, "If he wanted us, he would have come back by now. It's been years since he left. It does no good to think of Father." She drew her shawl more tightly around her shoulders.

Liam heard birds that he could not see, their twittering coming from deep in the gorse bushes along the road. Ahead, almost lost in mist that screened everything in sight, were two church spires—one Protestant and the other Catholic, St. Joseph's. The spires were so close they looked like fingers on one hand. Soon, St. Joseph's bells would ring and call people to Mass. In church, he would be obliged to take off his hat. People would think his hair had been cut off because of ringworm or lice. The boys who had captured him a week ago would like that.

During the Mass, people did stare at Liam. Afterward, leaving the church, he quickly clapped his hat back on his head. Just outside, the priest, Father Reilly, clasped Liam's hand and said he was glad Liam and his sister had come to the parish.

A rain had started to fall. Below the church steps, a child stomped his feet in muck, grinning up at Liam. The boy's mother tapped him on the head with her prayer book. "Jaysus," she said, "will you look at yourself, all covered with the mud?"

Ahead of Liam, tethered to a post, was Michael Lanigan's pony. Without her mane and flowing tail, hunched against the rain, she looked like a ruined thing. Liam wanted to go up to her but couldn't. He remembered how she had nuzzled at his hand when he fed her handfuls of grass by the stream.

It was then he was shoved from behind. One foot slipped into a puddle. "Watch your step now," a voice said, and again he was shoved. Now, both feet were in the puddle. He spun around and saw Colin, the gangly boy who had been with the others in the woods. Liam noticed what he had noticed then, ears that stuck out and freckles, some as large as coins.

Suddenly, from behind, hands clamped Liam's shoulders. He felt a knee in the small of his back. "Where is that knife of yours, Liam Tanner?" a voice asked. "I would like another turn with it myself. You had your turn, didn't you? A sorry sight my pony was when she came home last Sunday."

Then, somehow, Uncle Patrick was there. At once the hands let go. "Come along," Uncle Patrick said. Released, Liam simply walked straight after him.

Opposite the church were woods, and in the woods, on the other side of a stone wall, was a graveyard. Uncle Patrick trudged past, his pace the methodical pace of a workhorse in its traces. He said, "That lad is coming with us, I hope you know."

"Michael?"

"It was the two of them that did that to you? Taking the hair right off your head?"

Alice Ann caught up with them. She took one look at Liam's face. "What is it?" she demanded.

"Is it Michael Lanigan who is coming?" Liam asked Uncle Patrick again.

"The other lad, Colin, Mr. Gavin's son."

Mr. Gavin—he was the stranger then, the stranger who had sat on a stool in the cabin. He had said his son was coming.

"We'll have no animosity or fighting on our journey,

boyo," Uncle Patrick was saying. "Do you hear me? It is you I will hold accountable at any sign of that. It is not another whipping you desire, am I correct?"

"Answer, Liam, do," Alice Ann murmured when Liam said nothing. Kneeling next to him in the church pew fifteen minutes earlier, Alice Ann had passed a rosary through her fingers. It had glass beads. It was their mother's rosary. For a single instant Liam could hear in Alice Ann's voice his mother's voice—*Answer, Liam, do*. He put his hand in his pocket and touched the blue-gray stone from Mum's grave.

"I do not want another whipping," he told his uncle, but Liam could hardly swallow because his throat was crammed with the angry words he held back.

"And that means you will stay clear of Colin Gavin," Uncle Patrick said.

They walked on. On the outskirts of town, a pack of children played in front of a group of cottages. Ignoring the steady drizzle, they rolled an old bicycle wheel, poking at it with sticks to keep it moving. On the doorpost of one cottage was a horseshoe, and Liam was sure that a woman with a new infant had nailed it up to keep fairies away. She would fear that, if she didn't, a fairy would sneak into her cottage and exchange a fairy baby for her human one. No woman wanted a bad-tempered, irritable changeling. The woman in the cottage might break a new potato on the hearthstone and recite incantations to protect her baby from the fairies, too.

In America, were mothers afraid of fairies? Did people

think that a wailing banshee foretold a death? In a few weeks he would go. He would find that out.

He would go, but the shouting children would stay. These cottages would always be here, too, leaning close to one another, as if wanting company. It was the way cottages leaned together all over Ireland.

Five days later, Mr. Gavin came through the door to the cabin a second time. He almost filled it with his large frame. In his hands were boots. He held them up. "Brought these I have," he said to Uncle Patrick, "for your nephew, for America."

Uncle Patrick stood before a broken bit of mirror, which was propped on a small shelf. He mixed lather in a shaving mug. "Sure you shouldn't," he said by way of thanks. "None of your own can make use of them?"

Mr. Gavin set the boots on the stool by the table and said, "Too small they are for any of mine. Your lad is welcome to them."

Moments later Mr. Gavin left, saying he needed to return home. His terrier followed at his heels.

"Pack the boots up," Uncle Patrick said.

"If they belonged to Colin, I don't want them."

"Are you daft?"

"I will not wear Colin's boots," Liam insisted.

"Boots do not fall from the sky, and lucky you are to have boots at all," Uncle Patrick said. "And, the truth of the matter is, Colin never wore those."

"Whose were they then?" Liam asked.

"Full of questions you are at every turn and lacking in

sense altogether. Don't be getting above yourself. We've no need of your grand airs, boyo. Take the boots and be done with it!"

Uncle Patrick spoke while looking at his own face in the broken bit of mirror. And, as he often did when he was in his uncle's presence, Liam felt like an invisible being. He was a phantom, come to haunt this cabin, a phantom his uncle would like to be rid of.

Carefully Uncle Patrick ran a razor along the Adam's apple at his neck. Four-inches long, the blade was attached to a black handle. "Believe what I say. I am not in the habit of lying," he said to his own reflection. "They were not Colin's. Take the boots."

Liam crossed to the stool where Mr. Gavin had set them. He picked them up. The heels were run down, but the boots were well made. He ran the flat of his palm against the smooth leather.

"There's the mash for the turkey," Uncle Patrick said, "or have you forgotten your chores altogether? You will be giving that turkey its last meal, and the pullets, too. I have the innkeeper's promise to buy the lot, plucked and trussed and delivered this very day. And in two days time we will take the sow to market. "

Liam crossed the room. He put the boots inside the basket with his other belongings. Then, without warning, his uncle's bare feet were right by him. His feet were long, the toenails yellow and misshapen. The nails looked a century old.

When Liam glanced up, Uncle Patrick was wiping his razor clean with a scrap of rag. He could see the blade's bright edge. For one wild instant, Liam imagined that his uncle might put the razor to his throat, making him beg for his life. He told himself that he was as safe in this cabin as anywhere in Ireland. In spite of that, when Uncle Patrick's thumb glided along the razor, Liam took a quick, nervous breath.

"Do not ask Mr. Gavin where those boots came from," Uncle Patrick commanded. "It is none of your affair. Ask no one."

After Liam gave his word, his uncle moved away. Liam put a hand on the boots. He shouldn't ask where they came from. Why not? If they weren't Colin's old boots, who had worn them?

They departed in a small boat that would take them to Galway Bay, where they would board a great passenger ship for the Atlantic crossing. In the boat, along with Liam, were Mr. Gavin and Colin, Uncle Patrick and Alice Ann, and a redheaded girl Liam had never seen before. He guessed her to be sixteen, like Alice Ann. She glanced about her with a startled look, as if she'd never seen an oar or a wave or a gull.

The girl's mother ran along the shore. At the end of the beach she waded into the water, her arms held high above her head. If their father ever learned that Mum had died and if he searched for them, he might find Uncle Patrick's cabin and this beach, Liam thought. He might stand where this girl's mother stood. But then, like her, he would lose all trace of them.

The girl cried out, saying she would never see her

mother again. Mr. Gavin told her that she would. One day she would. Ignoring him, the girl started sobbing.

Out beyond the breakers, the steersman pulled his oars and set sails that filled to bursting in a stiff morning gust. As the boat moved forward, Liam told himself that he was not leaving his father behind. His father had gone ahead. He was in America already. If he had to search the new land from end to end, he would find his father and go to live with him. That was how he would escape from Uncle Patrick.

The girl no longer wept. She sat still, but her skirts billowed up in the wind. She smoothed the scarlet flannel down, stroking it over and over. She seemed to be trying to tame something wild. After that she did not look back. Liam didn't look back either.

CHAPTER FOUR

"HUGE AS THE SUN those stars may be, or bigger than the sun for that matter, any one of them," Mr. Gavin said. In the dim light that those stars cast, Liam could make out the ship's immense funnels and the second- and first-class decks above. Their own deck, the steerage deck, was empty, except for Mr. Gavin and himself. It was their fourth day on the water. At sunset, a storm had driven the steerage passengers below. By the hundreds, they slept there now in close-set bunks, or they tried to sleep through the hammering of the ship's engines.

Liam preferred the deck to that stinking hold, and so he had followed Mr. Gavin up the steps when Mr. Gavin asked if he would come along.

To Liam's surprise, Mr. Gavin seemed to want his company. When Uncle Patrick ignored him, Mr. Gavin might include him in their conversation. At any moment in the day, he might seek him out. Once he had showed Liam how to tie a half-hitch knot in a rope. Another time he had said the clouds they saw were cirrus clouds, and he'd described cumulus and nimbus clouds.

Mr. Gavin stood beside Liam now. His pointing finger slowly traced the great constellations in the northern sky. In the dark, Liam could barely see his face. He couldn't see his scraggily eyebrows or his full mustache, which was nothing like Uncle Patrick's thin, clipped one.

"God's handiwork we are seeing, you and I," Mr. Gavin said. "And God's realm it is, that sky. No other ruler holds sway there or ever will. No king or sultan will send his warriors off to fight there for a hill or for a valley."

"There were great Irish chieftains once, as great as kings or sultans, and great Irish warriors," said Liam.

"There were. Indeed there were. Always there are men who seek a battle out."

There was in Mr. Gavin's tone a note of disgust that puzzled Liam. He said, "But the chieftains were Ireland's heroes."

"It takes a battle to make a hero, is that it?" Mr. Gavin asked.

"Cuchullain claimed he did not care if he lived for only a day if his deeds lived after him. He was not afraid to fight or to die." In Irish myth, Cuchullain was Ireland's greatest warrior, so great that mortal men could not defeat him in battle, Liam knew. He died only when Queen Maeve's sorcerers lured him to his death.

"The Irish are brought up on mother's milk and tales of Cuchullain and his Red Branch Knights or Finn MacCool. Sure we love to hear of their grand battles." Mr. Gavin ended the speech with a dismissive snort.

"Uncle Patrick says he would have fought Cromwell's soldiers," Liam replied.

"Did he now? When Cromwell descended on Ireland with his terrible army, the Irish fought them to the death. Your uncle would have done that, a pike in his hand. Of that I have no doubt. And if I were there, those hundred and fifty years ago, I might have stood alongside him. There are times, don't you know, that give us no choice in the matter."

Mr. Gavin was as tall as any warrior, and as strong, but suddenly he said what no warrior would. "I hate to think, lad, of all I might have done, a pike in my own hand." He crossed his arms over his chest. "The chickens you and your uncle put to the knife last week, what if they were men? What of that?"

Blood had spurted when Uncle Patrick cut the throats of the chickens. He had given Liam the first one. While it was still warm, when its feathers came out most easily, Liam had plucked the creature. Next he had slit its belly and removed the guts. An hour later, nine chickens were dead. He had scrubbed his hands as hard as he could to get rid of the clinging odor of their blood.

"Chickens are not men," Liam said sharply.

"You do not want to think about the slaughter of men. And right you are. Sure it is a fearsome business, not a thing to glory in."

Liam looked into the murky night when Mr. Gavin fell silent. It seemed that the bitter wind was born in that dark place.

Mr. Gavin spoke over the wind, eyes on the sky.

"When I was just a lad in school, it was the stars I wanted to know about, and didn't the master bring me maps of the heavens especial. He would spread them out on the floor, and peruse them we would—as if we were bound to travel among the stars one grand day, as if we had to memorize our route for fear of getting lost among them."

Above them, sketched by stars, was Orion. Liam picked out the constellation himself. He picked out Ursa Major.

"A rude cabin it was, our school, with an Irish master who traveled from parish to parish to teach," Mr. Gavin was saying. "We would carry a sod of turf with us to put into the fire he kept against the cold."

He said nothing more until he said goodnight and left Liam.

Overhead, the stars seemed to shift in the heavens, but Mr. Gavin had said that the stars didn't move. It was the Earth that rotated on its axis. It felt, Liam thought, like the world was spinning under his feet at this very moment. As determined and headstrong as some great steed of Lord Clapham's, tossing its head and kicking, the world was giving him a ride.

Minutes later, when a figure appeared on the deck, Liam moved toward it, curious. It was Colin. He was gripping the rail. He groaned once and vomited into the sea. He straightened. At last, sensing he was watched, he turned his head.

"You," he said, "are you spying on me? Is that what you are about?"

"I'm not spying. Your father was here. He was talking about the stars."

"Da and his stars. He knows them all, from the books he reads. He says he would have been an astronomer, if Connemara lads ever did such things, but Connemara lads do not. Trinity College is not for the likes of us. Nor will it ever be, I am after thinking."

When Liam did not reply, Colin said, "I am under orders concerning you, Michael Lanigan's orders."

Liam already knew this. Each night there had been handfuls of sand in his bed. He assumed that the sand was carried all the way from the shores of Clifden at Michael Lanigan's command, and he suspected that Michael had given Colin a supply of pepper, too. Four mornings ago, his porridge was doused with pepper and he couldn't eat it. Last night, for the same reason, he couldn't eat his fish chowder. When Alice Ann had asked him what was wrong, Liam had only said that he wasn't hungry. Alice Ann had given him a peculiar look. "But you are always hungry," she had said.

Colin moved closer to Liam. "Michael gave me his orders. You will learn of them in time. I am to take care of you until we return and he is in charge again."

"Every day you vomit up your breakfast and your supper," Liam replied. "You are feeding half the fish in the ocean. They are trailing along after the ship, thousands of them, looking for their next meal."

Colin tried to slap his face. Liam ducked away and said, "A great storm is coming."

The storm was a lie Liam made up on the spot.

Colin said, "What do you know of it? What do you know of anything?"

"It will be a gale. A sailor told me," Liam insisted. "They are going to batten down the hatches and lock us below for days in the hold. And the ship will go mad, like nothing we have ever seen. In two days time, when the ocean is beating at the ship, we will be praying for our own salvation. The sailor told me that."

Liam heard Colin take in a great gulp of air and knew he was frightened. He said, "Are you going to be sick again?"

"I am not." Without warning Colin rushed Liam. He had him by his jacket. As it ripped open, Liam wrenched away. When Colin came after him, he lifted a leg. In the dark, Colin did not see it. He tripped and sprawled on the planks. Liam ran.

Once below, in the men's quarters, Liam crawled onto the thin mattress of his bunk and pulled a blanket up to his chin. Above him, in the top bunk, Uncle Patrick slept restlessly, shifting about.

There was a man—a thatcher from Sligo—who often shouted out at night. People said he was insane. They said he never should have been allowed onto the boat and that he would never be allowed into America. Now he stood and screamed out. Someone tried to hush him.

When Liam heard Colin descending the stairs to the hold, he rolled over and faced the wall. He knew that tomorrow Colin would say nothing of their fight. He wouldn't either. Somehow, without a word spoken between them, they had agreed on this when they could agree on nothing else.

Colin's bunk creaked as he climbed into it. Lips moving silently, Liam began his prayers. An hour ago, he had watched the stars. Traced on the black slate of the sky, they seemed like God's design. Such a God would not send a gale to make Colin vomit and vomit into the raging sea. Asking God for that would be a sin. But Liam hoped for a storm all the same because he and Colin were enemies.

The following morning, Uncle Patrick shook Liam awake. "You'll not sleep the day away," he declared. "Get up now." Uncle Patrick waited until Liam was sitting on the edge of his bunk before he walked away.

When Liam reached for his boots, he found that one was nailed to a floor plank. Angry, he pried it loose, examining the puncture in its sole. He put both boots on. Still he did not know who had owned them.

In coming days, his clothes were tied in knots. So were his bootlaces. Liam found a dead rat and put it in the cardboard suitcase that Colin kept below his bunk.

Through all of this, Mr. Gavin sought Liam out. Blinking owl-like the way he did, he talked about stars and clouds or sharks and lampreys. He knew all about such things, but Liam was forced to wonder if Mr. Gavin could see what was happening right in front of his eyes.

CHAPTER FIVE

Told that the ship would land in the morning, passengers were restless through the night, and before dawn, many were up. In the men's quarters, they crowded into the foul bathroom with its three toilets and two sinks, where they tried to clean themselves as best they could. Liam dipped the bottom of his shirt in the trickle of water from a spigot. He wiped his face with it and then tucked the shirt into his breeches. When he turned to go, a man with a turban jostled into his place, a razor in one hand and a mug filled with lather in the other. Outside the door, Uncle Patrick stood in a line of a dozen men. He clutched a bar of brown soap to his chest, as if he suspected that someone would try to steal it.

When Liam passed him by, Uncle Patrick said, "You'll wait for me by the galley-stove chimney. I've told Alice Ann to meet us there, and Mr. Gavin and Colin. We don't want to be separated, not in this rabble of people."

From below his bunk, Liam collected his things. He stuffed them helter-skelter into his lidded basket or into his rolled-up blanket, which he bound with twine. Ahead of him on the stairs, a man carried a huge black pot. Above him, three women struggled with a big feather quilt that slipped this way and that.

Once on the deck, Liam made his way to the galley-stove chimney and sat down to wait for the others. Nearby, seven men squatted in front of a gray-bearded man, who held a scribbled paper. Over and over this old man looked from the paper into their faces while he rattled off questions that would be asked at Ellis Island—questions about sponsors and wives and children and jobs and money and diseases and misdemeanors or crimes and politics. He waved his paper.

"Answer right. Answer the right way. Say what I say!"

In unison, all dutifully parroted his answers, except for one man, who stared silently at his clasped hands. Tugging furiously on his beard, the elderly man pointed at him. "Answer. Answer right, Abraham! Or back you go! Your other leg, you want they take that leg, too? Answer the questions!"

Who had taken off his leg? Liam asked himself. *Why?*

Just then, Alice Ann joined Liam. With two hands, she clutched her suitcase and said, "We're almost there. I can't believe it. I just can't." Her face was flushed with excitement. She put her suitcase down and sat on it, but she stood up again when Uncle Patrick appeared. Mr. Gavin and Colin were with him. Together, they moved toward the ship's bow. They took up positions at the railing, squeezing between others who were already there. Mr. Gavin took a place right beside Liam. A half-dozen feet away, Alice Ann and Colin and Uncle Patrick stood shoulder to shoulder.

In the distance was land. Closer and closer it came, until finally the ship entered a bay. There was a lighthouse on the right and swelling hills on the left. In front of them, a narrow passage led to a larger bay that contained three islands. As they approached the first, they saw a towering statue of a woman. She held a tablet in one hand and a torch in the other. She was wearing a crown. Mr. Gavin combed at his mustache with two fingers and straightened his jacket. It seemed that he wanted to make himself presentable for the woman's inspection, but she didn't notice Mr. Gavin. Her eyes searched the waters beyond, as if she had heard more ships were on their way and was looking out for them.

"The seven rays on Liberty's crown—there is one ray for each of the seven seas, for people ride the seven seas to seek her out." Mr. Gavin spoke quietly, but others shouted to the woman, as if she were alive. A man lifted a baby girl into the air, asking the statue to bless her.

"It was the French who gave her as a gift to the Americans," Mr. Gavin continued. "The French were friends to this nation during America's revolution. And friends they were to Ireland, when Ireland was fighting Britain for her own independence. Sure that is a thing you know."

"They came in ships," Liam replied, for he did know

that. "A French fleet landed in County Mayo. Another was turned back at Donegal."

"Aye, the French came a century and more ago and the French retreated, and little good Ireland gained from it, God knows. She still waits for liberty."

The boat continued across the calm waters. Near them now in the shifting crowd was a woman with a small girl, whose face was spotted and whose skin was a fevered red. A man in uniform was grasping the woman's arm. His voice rose. "Your child's infectious. Come away now. She should not be mixing with the others!"

The woman saw Mr. Gavin watching and cried out, "Her sister died three nights ago. They threw her into the ocean!"

As the uniformed man pulled the woman and child along after him, Mr. Gavin scowled at Liam. "Ah, a terrible thing it is," he said, "a child dying, and a sea burial into the bargain. Jesus, Mary, and Holy Joseph, now that is too much for anybody to bear."

As if someone had slapped him hard, Mr. Gavin threw back his head. "There was one of my own, don't you know, one that—" The sentence broke off. Mr. Gavin was silent for a moment. Then he crossed himself and said, "The matter is best left in the hands of God for I cannot bring myself to understand it. None of it."

Liam wanted to ask what had happened. Before he could, Colin wriggled in between him and Mr. Gavin. There he was with his ginger hair and the bones that jutted out from his narrow face—the sharp bone of his chin and his high cheekbones. Mr. Gavin slipped one arm around Colin's shoulders. To Liam, the arm looked like a strong rope that tied him to his son. They were father and son.

Deliberately, Liam ignored them. He watched a large steam ship instead. Dark smoke poured from its funnels, staining the blue sky. He listened to the lap of water and the shout from a sailing sloop twenty yards away. At the shout, he had a sharp memory. He was only four or five. A boy called Tom-Tom, the dairy-man's son, stood beside him in the doorway of an open horse stall. Tom-Tom had been trying to blow into a conch shell someone had lent them, but all that came out was a noise like huffing wind. It was then Liam saw his father. Striding across the stable yard, he struck a whip against bright, high leather boots and shouted out an order. It must have been winter, for Liam could see the breath of the boys in the air as they scurried to do whatever his father had told them to do.

That was his father, that proud, commanding man. Like Colin, he had a father still. Each day hundreds of ships swept into the harbor that lay in front of him. His father had come on one of them. He was certain of it, and Liam swore that he would find him. One day his own father would put his arm around his shoulders, like Mr. Gavin put his arm around Colin's shoulders. They would be father and son.

Pulled by tugboats, their ship drew nearer and nearer to New York City. Buildings jutted into the sky. They were so high it seemed they might topple over if tapped, like a soaring tower of child's blocks would. A river ran into the bay. Along it were long piers, with steamboats and sailing ships, tugs and barges plying the water close by. They came even nearer, so near that Liam could make out individual faces in the large crowd that awaited them. On one woman's head was a straw boater, its red ribbon fluttering in the wind. She had puffy cheeks and a rounded chin. She waved a parasol to the right and left with quick, determined movements. She seemed to be waving them down. As if obeying her order, the boat docked. The grating noise it made was like a howl.

Uncle Patrick and Alice Ann moved next to Liam. "Do we get off now?" Alice Ann asked him.

Liam didn't know, but a man next to Liam suddenly answered her question. "Not us," he said. "It's the first and second class passengers that get off here. We go back." He pointed to the island they had passed. "Back there is Ellis Island. You heard of the inspections?"

Uncle Patrick said, "All along, people have been talking about the inspections."

"Well, they inspect us on that island," the man told him, while plucking lint off the navy blue coat he wore. "They'll send a boat and take us over there."

"I don't see why they let the others off here without inspections, and not us," Alice Ann said indignantly. She looked up at the first-class and second-class passengers. On the decks above, they milled about.

In that crowd, Liam spotted the two men in black suits and derbies who had sometimes thrown apples or sugar buns or oranges over the railings to the children in steerage. They were tall, the two of them, and both had bright red hair and sharp features. Liam was certain they were brothers. One of them leaned over the railing now, waving to a few children, who looked up. Then the other flung a handful of coins into the air. The children scrambled for the money as it came flying down.

"That's why those folks don't need inspections," the man in the navy blue coat said. "They got so much money, they go and throw it away. They got places to stay in New York, too, and doctors if they get sick, and nobody's worried that they are going to be a burden."

A half-hour later these same first- and second-class passengers crowded the pier below. Swarms of stevedores and porters carried their trunks and their baggage. Cabbies waved them forward, onto a street jammed with traffic.

Excited, Liam watched. He longed to feel solid land under his feet, but a barge did not come for the steerage passengers until the sun had climbed into the sky. Herded forward by yelling men, they boarded this vessel. A gate slammed behind them. The barge chugged out into the harbor.

At Ellis Island, they were let off. Alongside Uncle Patrick, Colin, Mr. Gavin, and Alice Ann, Liam lined up in front of the entrance to the building he had seen hours ago from their ship. With its copper-domed turrets and its arches and parapets and brick walls, it looked like a fort. But a man in a fur hat was saying that the structure had been built to withstand a fire, not an army. He looked from one face to another, proclaiming that a previous edifice had burned to the ground, tumbling down in hours.

Two men passed out rolls. Famished—there had been no morning meal—Liam devoured his food. Colin did, too, while Alice Ann broke off small bits and popped them into her mouth.

When at last they entered the building, they were in a vast baggage room. There, people left bundles and satchels and suitcases before mounting wide, slate stairs. At the railing above, a doctor peered through his spectacles at a woman who stopped after a few steps to catch her breath. The doctor noted that the thatcher from Sligo was mumbling to himself. He saw Liam take advantage of an instant's opening in the mob, leaping two steps at once. The boy acted as if he were in a race, the doctor said to himself. He shoved his spectacles up on his nose. It was something he did when he was in an approving mood, although he was not ever aware of making any gesture of approval or disapproval at all.

The doctor's attention went from Liam to the hundreds and hundreds of others.

At the head of the stairs was a room that seemed as large as any field in Ireland. Light passed into it through high arched windows. When Alice Ann joined Liam there, they moved aside to wait for the others. "Someone scratched letters on the wall. Look," Alice Ann said. Her finger traced script carved into the plaster. "It is Arabic, I think."

They were like no letters Liam had ever seen. They were a stranger's alphabet. He looked about him. He saw a Chinese man who had a long pigtail and wore a small black cap. He saw a dark-skinned man, an African, in a dark blue robe. He saw a woman wearing a bright headdress and girls in swirling multi-colored skirts. He heard a dozen languages. If this was America, it was a stew of unlike peoples.

For hour after hour, they stayed in this building. They were made to join lines that inched slowly forward, past officials who glared at them or smiled, and who asked questions or demanded documents. Studying the ship manifest, one asked question after question, without ever bothering to glance their way.

"They treat us like cattle here," Uncle Patrick snapped.

The man snapped back. "Don't need nobody getting mouthy with me, mister." His eyes were still on his forms and not on Uncle Patrick. "You just move along like I'm telling you and do it quick."

Doctors examined them. When one lifted Liam's eyelids with a hook, Liam didn't protest. He clenched his mouth tightly shut. Done with the exam, Liam looked back at Colin to see if he would cringe when the hook poked his eyelid.

Colin saw Liam looking and didn't flinch either. He stood straight, like a soldier. Liam saw that his pants hung loosely on him. Too sick to eat during the ten-day crossing, Colin had lost weight. There were dark shadows under his eyes. Liam told himself that he was glad, because Colin was an enemy. He told himself that they would always be enemies, whether in Ireland or here.

Behind Colin, Alice Ann looked nervously at the man with the eyehook. Behind her, Uncle Patrick glared at him.

There were other doctors, who told them to cough or to inhale and exhale or to open their mouths and stick out their tongues. There were nurses, who ran hands through their hair, looking for lice.

After five hours, Liam stood in yet another line. Snaking forward between waist-high metal barriers, it seemed endless. In front of him, a woman yawned, a thin man rubbed at his temples to ease a headache, an old couple argued, and a baby wailed. Laughing, three little girls pressed their faces against the railing's iron bars. Liam shifted restlessly from foot to foot and wondered if this inspection would ever end. But twenty minutes later, arriving at the head of this line, he was given a card. He stared at the word printed on it—ADMITTED. He stared at a victorious Mr. Gavin, who waved his own card and who grinned at them. It was over. Uncle Patrick and Alice Ann and Colin and Liam all followed Mr. Gavin when he marched through a green door with its notice—PUSH TO NEW YORK.

The woman on the ferry dock was taller than any woman Liam had ever seen. Sighting them, she came forward. On her head was a big hat, and on that hat an olive green feather bobbed with each determined step she took.

She came closer. "Patrick Cavanaugh," she exclaimed, "is it truly you? And Molly's children—thank all that's good and holy!"

"'Tis Mrs. McCathery," Uncle Patrick said to Liam and Alice Ann.

When he said no more, the woman took up the introduction herself. A volcano of words erupted. "I was called Tess Eagan when I lived outside Clifden, long before Mr. McCathery ever set eyes on me or changed my name to his. Your mother was my cousin, but more like a sister back then. When we were little girls—four and five and six years old—why we would beg to spend a day together or a night sleeping in the other's cabin. In the morning she might be eating breakfast at my table, and in the evening I might be taking supper at hers. Siamese twins some called us. Grown as close as that we were."

Tess Eagan—it was the cousin their mother had often talked about. Liam knew her by that name. But, under a married name that he hadn't recognized— Mrs. McCathery—she had written to Uncle Patrick. It was her letter, Liam realized, that had come to Uncle Patrick's cabin, proposing that he come to New York.

They followed this Mrs. McCathery onto the crowded ferry that would take them to the city. At the end of the ferry's short journey, they followed her onto a dock and into a park. Dozens of trees lined the park's criss-crossing paths. Their leaves were coiled into tight, spring buds. Liam saw a fine lady, who twirled a parasol, and a scraggily man, who lugged a giant steamer trunk. On a bench stood a man, who told anyone who would listen about a double-your-money deal he was offering. He shouted and called. He waved a sheaf of papers at the bustling crowd of people to grab their attention.

"I'll have none of it," Mrs. McCathery said when he waved his papers at her. She clicked her tongue in disapproval. "They would take all you have if they could, these terrible hustlers they have here. Take all you have straight down to your undergarments." The disapproving click of her tongue turned into a laugh.

Mrs. McCathery pointed off to their left and said there was an aquarium in that direction. "It is called Castle Garden. Long ago, it was where I was examined, like you were today at Ellis Island. At the start it was a fort, and then an opera house, they tell me, and then it was the likes of me and Da and Ma coming through the door. After that, wasn't it the fishes that came? They keep them in great tanks. Why they swim around and around, getting nowhere at all, wondering how they came to be there." Again she laughed.

When they came to a street, Mrs. McCathery marched straight toward a young, dark-skinned man who stood there by a carriage. Standing by his side, she said proudly, "Oh, we could go home on the elevated or start off on the uptown trolley, but here is Mr. Hapwood with a carriage. He will take us home in proper style."

On Ellis Island, Liam had seen two men from Africa, the only black people he had ever seen. But where they wore brilliant robes, like kings might, this man was dressed in a worn coat that fell to mid-calf. Where they were old, he was only twenty-one or twenty-two, Liam estimated, with wide shoulders and an expansive chest.

But it was not the shoulders or chest that Liam noticed first. He saw first what anyone would—the scars. A large scar started at Mr. Hapwood's hairline and narrowed to a point just between his eyes. It had the shape of a spiraling flame. Another marked the entire left side of his face, from ear to jaw. Both had a reddish tint, the color of a smoldering blaze. It seemed they might ignite in an instant. His left eye was half-closed, little more than a slit. Liam did not know if he could see out of it.

As she said each one of their names, introducing them, Mrs. McCathery smiled. Mr. Hapwood didn't. He stood straight, staring from person to person out of his one good eye. He acted as if he were looking over a line of workman and boys before reprimanding them, the way Lord Clapham's strict head gardener might do.

When his eyes lit on Liam, Mr. Hapwood's good eye narrowed. His lips pressed into a tight line. Liam felt as if he were being accused of something—but of what? He had never seen the man before.

"Well, now," Mrs. McCathery said. She stepped into the carriage.

They followed her. Mr. Hapwood closed the door behind them. After a minute, the carriage lurched forward. Over the clamor of metal wheels, Mrs. McCathery said, "Our Mr. Hapwood, he has a way with horses that is uncanny. Animals—any animal at all—why Mr. Hapwood talks to them the same as he would talk to you or me, and they understand him, or seem to. I see him feeding pigeons, and the birds land on his outstretched arms. They are that easy with him."

There was a proud note in her voice. She could be talking about a favorite young relative, a nephew or cousin. Then she leaned forward, whispering, "The horse is his, but not the carriage. Oh, Mr. Hapwood borrowed the carriage to give us all a treat."

Mr. Gavin began talking to Colin in soft tones. Colin sat directly across from Liam. Their knees came close to touching but did not. When he saw Liam looking at him, Colin stared back angrily. He was telling Liam to look somewhere else, but Liam didn't, not until Colin finally looked the other way himself.

CHAPTER SIX

THEIR CARRIAGE TURNED OFF BROADWAY and onto
Fifth Avenue. Mrs. McCathery chattered about what
they were seeing—the Western Union Telegraph
Building and the Fifth Avenue Hotel. She pointed at a
restaurant called Delmonico's. "Mr. Hapwood's horse
pulled a fire wagon once upon a time, and the firemen
named him straight after that place—Delmonico he is
called to this day."

Why did she care about Mr. Hapwood or his horse?
Liam wondered. Wasn't he only a hired man?

The carriage rattled on. Mrs. McCathery's voice
rattled on, too. "See those grand houses there? They are
mansions, and they're owned by the Vanderbilts. And in
the train yards, not far at all from my very own building, you'll find a statue of the grandfather, Cornelius
Vanderbilt, who owned the trains. He was the one who
made a fortune to begin with."

They turned off Fifth Avenue and headed west. Block

by block, the scene changed. Gone were the carvings in stone and the statues, the marble columns, the brass trim, and the enormous display windows. Instead, plain buildings lined the streets. Gone were the men in frock coats and the women in fashionable dress. Instead, four children jumped rope in front of a scuffed sign that said *Get Fels Naptha Here*. Nearby, a fat man in a soiled apron stood guard over crates of cabbages and carrots and onions. At the corner, two young men crouched on the sidewalk, peering intently at a pair of dice one of them had tossed down.

The day was growing dim, as if, on these streets, light itself were being doled out in smaller and smaller quantities. Finally, the carriage pulled to the curb. "Ah, now we're home, safe and sound, and I'll show you to your rooms," Mrs. McCathery announced. "Mr. Gavin, you and your boy, you two will be staying with a widow who takes in boarders on the third floor, and the rest of you will go to the very top. It is a climb, but from up there you can look down at all the other rooftops, like the good angels looking down at the Earth below them."

Then she stepped briskly from the carriage. Uncle Patrick and Alice Ann went next. When Liam started to get up, Colin shoved him back. "After me, not before."

"I do not take orders from you," Liam replied.

Colin's long arm fixed him in place. "Never are you to go out of any door in front of me. Never."

Angrily, Liam followed Colin. As his foot touched the ground, Mr. Hapwood caught him by the elbow. Up close, Liam could see the strong tendons in his neck. For the first time, Liam noticed that half of his left ear lobe was gone.

"You know where you landed?" Mr. Hapwood asked.

Liam shook his head. Somehow that was what Mr. Hapwood wanted him to do, it seemed, because he nodded in approval. "They call it Hell's Kitchen, 'cuz right here's where the devil does his cooking. Go north or south and all the way over to the Hudson River—for blocks, it's Hell's Kitchen, and it's all his."

Mr. Hapwood spoke in a whispery voice, and Liam found himself straining to hear the words he did not really want to hear. "Better watch yourself. The devil's waiting to meet you. He is right out here, lurking about. He got his eye on you."

The scar on Mr. Hapwood's forehead shone. It could be the devil's brand, Liam thought, and he thought of Father Flaherty, the old priest who heard Confessions at St. Bridget's Church in Kildare. After Liam confessed his sins, Father Flaherty would always tell him that the devil lurked on Earth. One had to guard against him or he would snatch your soul away. Father Flaherty had unkempt hair and protruding eyes, like the eyes on Lady Clapham's pug dog. Liam and the other boys had always laughed at him. But now Liam remembered his warnings. With a sharp tug, frightened, he freed his arm from Mr. Hapwood's tight grasp. Mr. Hapwood gave a sharp laugh, like a dog's yap.

Liam's gaze darted from one thing to another as he stepped away. He didn't see the devil Mr. Hapwood claimed he would. What he did see were tired, sagging buildings. They were different heights—two, three, four, or five stories—and their roofs made an uneven line against the sky, like a monster's jagged teeth. With night coming on, the windows that were lit up became the monster's bleary, yellow eyes. A rooster sat on a fence post. It crowed at Liam, ruffling its feathers. Down the block, strung on uneven posts, another fence staggered back and forth, as if it were drunk. Between two buildings five men crouched together. They tossed slats from a crate onto a fire.

Alice Ann waited for Liam in the doorway, a fearful look in her eyes because she had just seen all that he had. "It's an awful place," she whispered. "Those men and all the trash and that stench. The pile of manure at the curb is as high as my head."

Together, they entered the building. High above them, Liam could hear Mrs. McCathery's voice singing out. "Now Mr. Gavin, you and Colin will be in these rooms. Go explore a bit while I show Patrick the garret apartment."

Liam heard a door close and looked up the stairwell, where, suddenly, Mrs. McCathery's head appeared. She was leaning over a banister and waving at them and calling, "Ah, there you two are. Come along now. You'll be at the very top! Follow us!"

Liam shouldered his blanket and clutched the heavy basket, then started up the uneven, dirty steps. From below came the sound of Alice Ann's reluctant footsteps and the bumping of her suitcase against the banister. She was terrified by the dark look of the place. He thought of how, only minutes before, Mr. Hapwood had tried to terrify him.

Then Liam remembered how, in Kildare on hot summer days, he and the other boys would ride the tearing current of a stream. At points the water might pull him under, like an unexpected hand yanking him straight down. Then he would surface, gasping for air, listening to the sharp calls of the other boys.

He had never been afraid to jump off high rocks into that cold, fast water. Mr. Hapwood could not make him afraid of whatever ride was coming now, no matter what he said or did.

At dawn, standing at the garret windows, Liam watched a train of a dozen cars that ran along high, elevated tracks, cinders flying behind it. It seemed that the train and the morning sun burst into life in the same moment.

"Liam, come," Alice Ann called. She spooned oatmeal into three bowls set along the edge of the coal stove. She gave one to Uncle Patrick, who sat down on the one and only chair. Last night he had slept in the only bed. Except for a handful of dishes, a scuttle of coal, and the two chamber pots Mrs. McCathery had provided—so they wouldn't have to go down the dark stairs and out to the backyard privy in the middle of the night—that bed and chair and the two thin mattresses Liam and Alice Ann had slept on were the apartment's only furnishings.

There was barely space for anything more. The

apartment was narrow and the front room and the single bedroom were small. But because it was a garret apartment, the ceilings were high, and along one wall of the front room, tall windows let in bright morning light. The light played tricks, making the room seem bigger than it was.

"In need of a scrubbing, this place is," Uncle Patrick said. He studied the rips in the linoleum and the stained wallpaper, and the clumps of dust and dirt that were everywhere. "I don't know who lived here before us, but surely they left us a pigsty."

He scraped up the last of his porridge and said, "The two of you will set about fixing that, and I'll want a dinner when I come home as well. Nothing fancy, mind. I've no money for fancy vittles, but you'll buy what we need. You'll find where we're to get coal. Set the place in order you will." He drew two bills out of his vest pocket. He held them out, nodding at Alice Ann, who stepped forward and took them.

When she stepped back, their uncle gulped his tea. He stood and put a cap on his head. "Mrs. McCathery is sending me off to a man by the name of Mister George Washington Plunkitt, a politician who runs affairs in this district, with a hand in everything that happens, she says. She promises that he'll find work for Mr. Gavin and myself. She's already spoken to him. This morning he'll see us." He stared at Liam. "Next you'll be finding work, boyo. You'll be out looking for a way to earn your keep." He looked at Alice Ann. "The both of you."

Alice Ann nodded. She said, "Mrs. McCathery said

she talked about me to a man who runs a pharmacy. It's a block from here. I can go to see him, Uncle."

"Well, tomorrow will be soon enough for that, or the day after." He scowled at the room. "First you're to make this place habitable. Mrs. McCathery says she will lend you a broom and mop and bucket, and you are to talk to her about furniture. She has some stored away. Liam, you will go and see her."

"There will always be a place for you here, and don't you be forgetting that," Mrs. McCathery said when Liam stepped into her apartment an hour later. She wiped her hands on her apron. Today, in place of the shiny striped skirt she had worn on the Ellis Island dock, was a plain brown one. Here and there, small stains dotted the material.

She led Liam into her kitchen, sat him down at the table, and poured dark tea into the cup she set in front of him. She moved a kerosene lamp to make room for a pitcher of milk and a bowl of sugar. "Add what you will," she said.

Instead of telling Mrs. McCathery that he had already eaten one breakfast, Liam watched her slap a rasher of bacon into a pan. He had not smelled sizzling bacon since he left Lord Clapham's house.

Mrs. McCathery was talking about going with Mum's family, when they were little girls, to Croagh Patrick, the hill above Clew Bay. "We went for the July pilgrimage, in honor of Saint Patrick. It was a long, long journey, but it was perfectly grand. I know your uncle never took you there, but did he ever take you to Saint Patrick's holy well or Saint Caillin's well? They are just beyond Balyconneely, not far."

"He took us nowhere at all," Liam replied.

"Well, Patrick Cavanaugh is not a traveling man," Mrs. McCathery declared, laughing. "Why yesterday, didn't I guess as much? The merry world rolling by and Patrick Cavanaugh not ever looking out the carriage window."

She drew a breath, enough for her next surge of words. "But for all that, he is right about many things, about all the English did when they took Ireland for their own." She swept straying hair aside with the back of her hand. "In those times the English made each and every law. Catholics couldn't vote. We had no say in anything. They told us we could not sell our fine Irish wool or linen to other lands, or even lamb and fish. England was to have all the trade. They left us no way to earn our keep, and when we were crippled entirely, the famines came. Why, the poor had nothing to eat and no way to pay their rent. After that, the landlords drove them out, setting torch to thatch and burning the cabins down." Her face flushed with the heat of her own words.

"Oh, your uncle is correct. Correct in everything he says, and an upstanding man, only . . . " Mrs. McCathery let the sentence trail away.

Then she said, "Patrick Cavanaugh is Molly's brother, and he is more than an uncle to you now." She searched Liam's face, waiting, Liam thought, for some kind word from him about his uncle. He could not bring himself to say anything.

Finally, Mrs. McCathery spoke again herself. "At the very last I had a letter from your mother. She wrote to say she would send you to your uncle when she died. She asked that I talk with people in the Irish societies here. There are dozens of them—with all the Irish that live in this city! They often give a warm welcome to men from Ireland who are fighting for the republican cause—for freeing Ireland from English rule. Your uncle and Mr. Gavin have been involved in that side of things since they were no older than you are now."

Her voice dropped lower. "It can be a frightful business. The men in one of these Irish associations, the Clan na Gael, why they buy weapons. They are looking to fight. Nobody involved in such affairs would ever speak of the particulars to you or to me, of course."

In her pan, the strips of frying bacon made a spitting noise when Mrs. McCathery pushed them from side to side. "Some will do anything at all to make England give up Ireland for once and all. And here I am myself, taking a hand in it. I did what Molly asked. I made arrangements, and then I lured Patrick Cavanaugh here. Why, four nights from tonight, on Saturday night, your uncle and Mr. Gavin will be speaking at Hibernian Hall, at a meeting of the Irish Federation of America. They are sending Colin out to put up posters to announce it. Did you know they were going to talk?"

"Uncle Patrick hasn't said anything about it," Liam replied.

"Well, he will give a speech. And all because of your own mother and myself. Months ago, she told me to do what I could. It is not chance alone that brings you and Alice Ann to this city. Do you understand what I am saying to you?"

Mrs. McCathery looked at him, and Liam said, "Mum never wanted us to stay with Lord Clapham. I know that."

He remembered Mum coming out to the orchard to tell him this. He was high in a peach tree, pruning it. He had descended the ladder, and Mum had leaned against it, taking quick breaths and telling him that he and Alice Ann would go to Connemara when she died.

"Connemara, it is not like here," she had said. "When I was a girl, I loved it. I think of your being there, not here on Lord Clapham's land, of Alice Ann's being there, not here." She had looked almost disapprovingly at the hundreds of fruit trees, which paraded, side by side, in long, perfectly straight rows. "It is wild there, Liam, not like this at all."

Liam had seen what Mum meant when, at the end of the train ride that took him and Alice Ann across Ireland, the sun-streaked Connemara hills came into view. They seemed to leap up from the ground. A mist sidled up to them, nosing them like a wandering fox would nose some new find. The sky was crossed by unruly clouds and tinged by blood-red light because the sun was starting to set.

"Mum said she loved Connemara," Liam said. "She hoped we would."

Mrs. McCathery was stacking bacon on a plate and putting bread in the pan to fry it and saying, "Molly always missed it. But she was never sure it would be right for you in the end." She stepped to the table and took a sip of tea from her cup. She put it down. "Truthfully, she wasn't sure about Patrick either, about your uncle."

"Mum wanted me to come here. Is that what you are saying?" Liam asked.

She nodded. "You will make your own choice in time. Until then, why won't I do everything I can for you and Alice Ann?" She brushed the back of his neck with her hand. Her quick touch was so like his mother's that it startled Liam. It made him want Mum back again.

Then Mrs. McCathery returned to her cooking. With her back to Liam, she said, "All through the years, distant as we were, your mother and I stayed close. Letters there were, certainly, a steady stream of them, so we would never lose track of one another. And all these years I kept her letters by me. Of course I would."

Without thinking, he blurted out, "Did she write you when my father left? Do you know where he is?"

Mrs. McCathery swung about, a startled look on her face, as if Liam had given her a prod with a stick. But she said nothing.

"Is he alive at least?" Liam asked. "Do you know that?"

No answer came. Liam hunched over his tea.

"Well, he was your father after all," he heard her murmur finally. "Yes, he is alive, and prospering—or was when your mother wrote to me about him. She said he prospered."

"Prospered where? Where is he?"

"It is not for me to say. I should say nothing at all. Your mother would have none of it, Liam."

No one would speak of his father. He did not know why. But once, Liam realized, his mother had revealed everything—in her letters to Mrs. McCathery.

Suddenly, he was hunting for any sign of them. On the crowded kitchen shelves were canisters and jars, cast-iron muffin pans, earthenware crocks, teacups and plates, and three flat irons with wooden handles. There were odd things, too. An empty birdcage sat on the floor in the corner. A copper vase held a single peacock feather. On a little table were miniature statues of cats, each playing a different musical instrument.

But precious letters would not be kept in someone's kitchen.

Less than an hour ago, when Mrs. McCathery had let him in, she had shown him her parlor, where her two boarders slept. One used the sofa, and the other used three kitchen chairs set side by side at night to support a narrow mattress stuffed with cotton. He and Mrs. McCathery had passed from the parlor and along a short corridor to this kitchen. On the way, they had walked by a closed door. Behind it would be Mrs. McCathery's bedroom. Liam longed to search that room.

Mrs. McCathery was setting two plates piled high with food on the table. She sat down across from Liam, who immediately devoured three strips of crisp bacon. He loved the very crunch of it between his teeth and the pungent taste. When he looked up, he saw that Mrs. McCathery was watching him. "Ah, I'm glad to see a boy with a hearty appetite," she said, grinning. She cut off a corner of fried bread, spiked it with her fork, and asked, "Do you know how I make my living then, that I can dally at home in the morning like this?"

"You take in two boarders."

"You will meet my boarders tonight, but what they give me in rent, why that barely keeps me in tea and bacon." She leaned forward. "There is money in miracles, don't you know, and so I perform miracles! That is how I earn my keep."

Mrs. McCathery laughed at the look Liam gave her. "I perform miracles of stitchery—a miracle with needle and thread. Why, after an hour or two in my hands, a gown brought two years ago from Paris is fashionable again. Oh, and can't I make a stout matron appear slender, with a twist of cloth here or there? Why certainly I can!"

On the wall to her left was a picture of Jesus. Eyes on Liam, Jesus seemed to be ordering him to think no more about the letters. But Liam found he was looking down the corridor to her bedroom.

"Uncle Patrick said you knew where we could find a table and chairs," Liam said to Mrs. McCathery as she cleared away their plates.

"Years ago, the man who owns this building said that I could have any belongings people left behind when they moved from here," Mrs. McCathery answered. "Renters sometimes leave a thing or two, especially when the rent is long overdue and they are sneaking away at three or four in the morning because they don't want to pay it." She winked at Liam.

Mrs. McCathery put dishes in the sink and returned with a rag. Sweeping up crumbs, she scrubbed the table. "Mr. Hapwood helps me," she continued. "We take what leavings there are, and Mr. Hapwood stores them in his stable, in a little room he keeps locked up. We sell some things. We give half of it away. Certainly your uncle can have any of it."

Mrs. McCathery led Liam into the corridor. Liam followed her through a back door and onto a rickety porch.

From there, to the east, he could see the elevated tracks that hurtled across the sky above Ninth Avenue. To the west were tall brick structures. Mrs. McCathery followed Liam's gaze and said, "Over there, you will find the warehouses and stables and slaughterhouses and tanneries. And beyond that, the railroad and the Hudson River itself."

Liam saw short apartment buildings and tall ones, and he saw tumbledown shacks. Some yards had gardens; trash filled others. Buildings might crush together but suddenly open onto a vacant lot. In one of those lots, two pigs snuffled about. Tethered to a post, a goat bleated for all it was worth.

This world was a jumble of unlike things. It seemed to Liam that some great giant, whose head touched the sky, had pitched everything out here onto the ground with one haphazard swing of his arm, not caring where any of it landed.

Mrs. McCathery was looking about, too. She gave Liam her wide grin. "There is no knowing who you will meet next on these streets or what language they'll be speaking or if you'll understand a word of it. But neighborly we are, for all that—for the most part, we are. People stay put, or if they move, they move a block or two away from where they started. I know half of them by now."

Slumped in one corner of the yard was a privy. The wind carried its smell. In that wind Mrs. McCathery's skirt flew backwards. "A March wind is blowing still, whether it's April or not," she said cheerfully. Liam buttoned his coat against its sting, as Mrs. McCathery pointed. "Just go through the lot there and the empty yard beyond, where Mr. Hapwood pastures his horses. And beyond that, see that old barn? Mr. Hapwood uses it for a stable. If he hasn't left to make his deliveries, he will be there. He can give you a key to the storage room."

Liam remembered Mr. Hapwood's left eye, which drooped while he stared hard out of the right one. And there had been the blistering scars. Mrs. McCathery gave Liam a nudge, casting him out into the frigid day. "Be quick or he'll be gone. Off you go!"

Mr. Hapwood had said yesterday evening that Liam was in the devil's land. In his whispery voice, he had seemed to be calling the devil up. Liam wanted nothing to do with him.

"Didn't I say you would just catch him? Run!"

CHAPTER SEVEN

Without a sound, Liam slipped into Mr. Hapwood's stable. He stepped sideways and stood against the wall. The air smelled of horse and alfalfa and straw and manure and linseed oil and leather. At the very first breath, Liam could imagine he was in Kildare again, ready to take a horse from its stall. At that first breath, he felt happy.

But it was not Kildare. Mr. Hapwood was here. In the middle of the stable, he was hitching a tan horse to a wagon. A shaft of light fell across Mr. Hapwood's right side but not his left. He was both bright and dark, a man split in two.

A minute passed. As his eyes adjusted to the dimness, Liam made out a second horse, this one in a stall. He was as gray as the stable's gray light. He twisted his head to look at Liam and stamped a hoof, warning him to keep his distance. Curled beneath his belly was a yellow dog, which didn't bark at him or stir at all, making Liam think the dog was old and deaf.

And then Mr. Hapwood's voice rattled out. "What you doing back there? You, Liam Tanner, you come out of there."

Hesitantly, Liam stepped away from the protection of the wall. Mr. Hapwood had not once looked up. How had he known he was there? He watched Mr. Hapwood tighten the breeching strap on the tan horse's harness. When the horse moved his legs, dust spiraled up from his hooves and caught in Liam's throat. He coughed. Mr. Hapwood said, "This here animal pulled a fire wagon before I got hold of him. Don't look like much now maybe, but he is still some animal. Keeping a low profile nowadays is all."

Mr. Hapwood's voice was the voice Liam remembered from yesterday, a whisper, yet not a whisper. "Pays to keep a low profile in this world. The horse and me, both of us been doin' just that." Mr. Hapwood grinned. It was a grin that Liam did not like because it seemed to mock him. In Mr. Hapwood's eyes he was just an Irish boy, who was small for his age and who knew nothing of life here.

"So, are you a judge of horse flesh?" Mr. Hapwood asked Liam. He asked that with a calculating eye, as if the question were a test. Liam only nodded, but he wanted to say that he had watered and fed horses and groomed them all his life and that he always wanted to be near them. He wanted to say that he would slip onto a horse's back whenever he could and that he had never been afraid, no matter how big the animal was.

Once, when he was only nine or ten, boys had dared

him to ride Morengo, the master's piebald stallion, who had white markings around his right eye and brown markings around his left, giving him a crazy, clownish look. Liam hadn't been afraid to ride him, though he was so small at the time that he could hardly reach the creature's back to saddle him up. On horseback, in the middle of the night, he'd traveled through miles of woods to the stream head where the boys were waiting. They had surrendered the things they promised they would give him if he ever came — a slingshot and marbles and whips of licorice.

In Kildare, Lord Clapham's hunting stable had towering rafters and large horse stalls that faced a cobbled courtyard. It was three or four times the size of this stable, and not piled everywhere with junk like this one was. In Kildare, there were no old wheels, no scraps of lumber, no dented lady's bicycle, no pile of newspapers, no barrels filled with cans and rags, like here.

Liam came closer to Mr. Hapwood's horse. He had a thick chest and strong legs. His tan coat shone. At his fetlocks and muzzle, the tan turned to black. Liam stole another look at Mr. Hapwood, who was not half as well groomed as the animal. The vest he wore was covered with bits of straw.

As Liam thought that, Mr. Hapwood brushed the straw off his jacket and stared at him. He stared so hard, it seemed he was looking right into his mind.

Liam had heard that some people could do that, gypsy tinkers or the black arts men who performed their magic at fairs. Could Mr. Hapwood read minds, too?

"What you come for?" Mr. Hapwood asked.

Liam opened his mouth to answer Mr. Hapwood's question but stopped when he heard a whirring noise. A pigeon shot out from the rafters. It flew up and hung in front of a high window, wings beating frantically. Mr. Hapwood looked up. "You come down from there, dang bird," he said. "No way out up there." At once, the pigeon did what it was told, diving down.

He could talk to animals, Mrs. McCathery had said. Could Mr. Hapwood cast spells on them so they'd immediately submit to him like this?

Mr. Hapwood said, "What do you want, I asked you."

When Liam told him that Mrs. McCathery had sent him for a key, Mr. Hapwood fetched a ring of keys out of a trouser pocket. He plucked one off. "If she says you folks can take whatever furniture you want, that's fine by me."

He eyed Liam. "You make your way over here all right? Through the yard? The man out there, the one who lives in the tent out there, why he's got quite a reputation. Used to be a big man in one of the gangs 'round here, called the Gophers. He got hit in the head once too often with a mallet or a bat or a chain or some such. Now he's crazy as a loon."

Coming here, Liam had passed by a tent in the yard, but he had not seen a man.

Mr. Hapwood did not light the pipe he extracted from inside his vest. Clamping it between his even teeth, he sucked air through it, and when he spoke, his words sputtered. "You go by him, that man is bound to say how he'll hit you in the head. You keep your eye out for him. See if I'm not right about that."

Liam watched Mr. Hapwood fill a feedbag and place it in the wagon next to jugs of water. On the side of the wagon hung a sign that read *Hapwood & Co., Transport*. Mr. Hapwood seemed too young to own a transport company all his own, unless it consisted of this one wagon and one horse.

As if bawling him out for having such a thought, Mr. Hapwood called over to Liam in a sharp voice. "You gonna open those doors for me or am I gonna do it myself? You gonna be of some help?"

"I will," Liam answered. Mr. Hapwood mounted his large wagon then. He took the reins in his hands. Liam pushed at the stable doors, which opened, creaking. Outside, he noticed a small furrowed garden and the scarecrow that guarded it. The scarecrow was clad in red, ragged long johns.

"Close those doors for me," Mr. Hapwood ordered. As Liam did, the wagon clambered over uneven stones that led to the street.

When Liam started back the way he had come, through the gate of the yard and into the empty lot, a man stood before the entrance to the tent. Like Mr. Hapwood's scarecrow, he too wore long johns. Like the scarecrow, he had scrawny legs and stick-like arms. He was drinking out of a tin can. As Liam passed, this scarecrow of a man took one lurching step forward. Suddenly his voice rose, shrill as a whinny. The words that followed startled Liam—"You come near me, I'm gonna hit you in the head. Hear me?"

How could Mr. Hapwood know the scarecrow man would say exactly that?

Liam ran, as much from Mr. Hapwood and his strange powers as from the scarecrow man.

When Liam was going up the stairs, he met Colin, who was coming down. Colin elbowed him hard, shoving him against the banister. "You'll not get away from me, you know," he said. "You'll not escape. I'll always be here."

Liam shoved him back. Only then did he notice the boy who stood on the turning of the stairs above them. He'd stopped, his brown eyes full of interest, as if he were watching a scene in a play.

Colin looked up and saw him, too. "Another time then," he grunted. As he started down the steps again, Liam went up.

"A friend of yours?" the boy asked in an ironic tone. He had curly black hair, which spilled over a high forehead. He brushed it out of his eyes.

"Not a friend, no."

The boy looked Liam over, examining him from head to foot. He was someone who would want to know everything about everyone, Liam decided. When the boy grinned, Liam felt like he'd just passed a test of some kind. "Well, he's a head taller than you, and older than you, but you stood up to him," the boy declared.

"Name's Jacob." He held out his hand, and when Liam shook it, he said, "I live right below you. My ma said she saw you moving in. Before you, there were six or seven men living there, and they'd hoot and holler half the night, and throw their trash right out the window, so you'll be an improvement." Standing straight, his head cocked to the side, he seemed sure of himself. "Ma was glad to see a girl, too. Your sister?"

Liam nodded.

"And he's your dad, the man?"

"My uncle," Liam told him.

"Well, see ya," Jacob said, "got things to do and places to go." He had a wild, lop-sided grin. A half a floor away, head turning, he called up the stairwell, "See you around!"

That night Uncle Patrick washed at a sink that was out in the hallway, splashing water at the dirt on his face. His shirt off, he rubbed at his chest with a wet rag. Liam handed him the towel he'd been told to fetch.

"We found work all right," Uncle Patrick said. "All day we went at it, laying pipes in the street, and the foreman is not what I'd call a gentleman. I'll tell you that. Pushes the men, he does, pushes them beyond exhaustion." He dried his wet face. Tired lines crossed it. "Tomorrow you will find work. You'll go up and down these streets, asking for a job, and you'll take a job with anyone who will have you. Once you are working, you will give every penny straight to me to pay for your keep."

He pulled a stained undershirt over his head. He picked up a blue work shirt that lay on a stool by the sink, held it in his hand, and said, "I will collect money for Ireland herself—Saturday night Mr. Gavin and myself will start our campaign. We're to talk in a grand hall they've got here. But the money I make working, with that foreman wearing me out, that money goes to Connemara land. I'll not be breaking my back to pay your way."

As he glowered at Liam, Liam took a step back. "Yes, Uncle," he answered. Only then did Uncle Patrick put on his shirt, still observing Liam with distrust.

The next day Liam scrubbed in the sink, like Uncle Patrick had done the night before. He slicked back his hair. With a wet rag he attacked the spots of dirt on his trousers and then put on his one clean shirt.

"You look presentable," Alice Ann said. She stood in the doorway, a bucket in one hand and a scrub brush in the other. "Someone will hire you. You'll see. For now, there is dirt enough for me right here, but tomorrow I'll go to that pharmacy, and if that Mr. O'Donnell hires me, then we'll all be working."

When Liam went down the stairs, Alice Ann called after him. "Liam! Stop by Mrs. McCathery's. If she's still there, ask if she can leave the stove-blacking polish outside her door for me. She said I could use it."

On the first floor, Liam knocked at Mrs. McCathery's door. There was no answer. He knocked more loudly. Still no answer came, and he decided that Alice Ann would have to borrow Mrs. McCathery's polish another day.

To get his bearings before setting out, Liam went through the narrow back door to the building and onto the porch, where he'd stood the day before with Mrs. McCathery. Once again, he looked to the east, toward the elevated tracks. Above them hung clouds that were as thick and dark as lead. He looked to the west, toward the river and the docks. He had to search for work in this new, strange land, but where should he start?

Wary and reluctant, Liam leaned for a moment against the porch railing. Looking back at the building, he saw a window that was slightly open in Mrs. McCathery's first-floor apartment. Just below it was a thick post, one of six that propped up the back of the building. He knew he could shinny up it. He could climb through the window.

In the apartment were Mum's letters. They had to be there.

He thought that, and before he could think again—thinking might stop him—Liam ran down the back steps. The next thing he knew, his knees were locked around the post. He pulled his body upward. Then he was shoving at the window with one hand, supporting himself with the other. Little by little, the opening in the window widened.

At the very last, before slithering through, Liam looked behind him to make sure that nobody watched him. All that he saw were five crows that flew up from the roof of Mr. Hapwood's stable, cawing loudly.

Inside Mrs. McCathery's parlor, Liam took one step forward, and a board creaked. Alert for any answering sound, he held his breath. No one was here, he told himself. Not Mrs. McCathery. Not the boarder with the missing teeth, who worked in the sugar refinery on Eleventh Avenue and left the house when it was barely light. Not the other boarder, the tinsmith who stuttered when he talked. He was alone.

Still Liam's heart beat faster as he crept into the hall-way that led to the kitchen. Along it was the door to Mrs. McCathery's bedroom. If he opened that door, would he find Mrs. McCathery in bed, a cold cloth held on her forehead because of a fever? She would give a startled cry and sit up and ask him what on Earth he was doing, and he would say that... he would say he had knocked and when she hadn't answered, he—

Through the small crack that opened when he pushed at the door, Liam peered at a bed. It was empty. He stepped inside. The tiny room had a tin ceiling, stamped into decorative squares. On the floor, covering rough planks, was an oval braided rug. A small chest of draw-ers stood against the wall. Over it, a silver pocket watch hung from a hook.

Liam reached a hand out and turned the watch over. Inscribed on the back was a man's name, Silas McCathery. He must be Mrs. McCathery's dead hus-band, Liam realized. She had told him only yesterday of his dying in a fire. Before he did, he'd brought a dozen people out. The watch ticked, which meant she must wind it. Next to it, pinned to the wall, was a plait of dark hair. Woven into a circle like a bracelet, it would be Silas McCartney's hair, kept as a remembrance. There was a picture inside an oval frame, too. Silas McCathery held a wide-brimmed fire helmet to his chest. Nostrils flared, he seemed to be testing the air for smoke.

He had no time for watches and pictures and Silas

McCathery. He began opening drawers, his hands sorting swiftly through Mrs. McCathery's belongings. In two wooden boxes, ventilated with tiny holes, were soft leather gloves. There was a paisley shawl and stockings and a bag full of long, sharp hatpins.

Liam saw no sign of the letters.

When he searched a narrow armoire, he found the red shoes Mrs. McCathery had worn on the Ellis Island dock. A jacket hung on a peg. Quickly he opened a hatbox, and then another. It was in the third hatbox that he found the letters, tied with ribbon. He grabbed them up. There were dozens of letters, too many to read in the time he had.

But what if the letters were in order? If they were, the letter at the bottom of this pile would be the very first that his mother had written; the letter on top, the last. And the letter she had no doubt written to Mrs. McCathery when his father left? Liam stared at the stack, judging that single letter's position.

Carefully he untied the sky-blue ribbon. He slipped the bottom-most letter out. The address on the envelope was written in a child's hand. Inside was his mother's first letter then.

Into the room's silence came a rapid tapping at the window. Liam's heart jumped. When he turned, he saw that drops of water struck the pane.

That was all it was—rain. On the porch, minutes ago, he had seen the sky's dark, sagging clouds. Now this rain spilled from them, and wind flung the drops. Still, it was as if the rain's tapping were a warning, someone's telling him to run. He drew a letter out of the pile. He slipped it from its envelope and read the date — 9th of July, 1891. Had his father left before that date or after? He didn't know.

He scanned the page, searching for the telltale words — *my husband* or *the children's father* or *William. . . .*

He saw other words — *Bridget O'Brien has had her baby, but he is a peaked little thing.. an entire setting of crystal sent from Waterford. . . . the mistress is most dissatisfied with little Fanny, and I do suppose Fanny will be sent back to that awful father of hers before I can to train her out of her slovenly habits and into proper ones. . . .*

All was written in his mother's curling script. His mother had been very proud of her fine hand. She would dip the nib of her pen into the inkbottle and carefully copy favorite passages from her Bible. She would slip the passage into a frame she had hung on the wall for that purpose. For some reason no one stopped her from doing that, although servants were not supposed to keep decorations of any kind on the walls of their rooms.

Silently Liam replaced that letter. He raced through the next with his eyes, the way he might race over flat ground with his feet.

He had opened four letters. It was in the fifth, grabbed impatiently and almost at random from the pile, that Liam found his father's name. *William says that he would stay if given the choice. How can he want that? And after the great, grand lies he has told me all this while, how can I believe any thing he says?* This is what Liam's mother had written.

I don't know what I can do. Lady Clapham . . .

A sound registered somewhere in Liam's conscious-
ness, but his eyes were on the words—*Lady Clapham is
not one to abide scandal. Sure she will ask William to go and
what of us then? On that I cannot think.*

Scandal—Liam's eyes slid backwards to that word and
then went forward again. When a key turned in a lock,
he did not hear it.

*On that I cannot think. Never can I go with William if he
is sent away. Knowing what I now know, how could I ever . . .*
A voice brought Liam to attention. "Soaking wet you
are." That was said loudly and with a laugh, Mrs.
McCathery's laugh. A door banged shut, the front door.
There came the sound of footsteps along the hallway.
After a moment, from the other side of the wall that
separated this bedroom from the kitchen, came voices.
The wall was so thin that Liam could hear half of what
was said— ". . . and don't they go to Paddy's Market
every day or twice sometimes in hopes . . . "

Frantically, Liam shoved the letter under his shirt and
into his waistband. He did the same with the letter above
it and the one below it in the pile, and then, suddenly, he
grabbed two from the very top. They would be the last
his mother had written.

As he shuffled the remaining letters into a neat stack, he
heard Mrs. McCathery say—"It was those potatoes that
weighed me down the most, like a donkey with its load."

Liam's fingers fumbled with the ribbon, tying it.
Someone was telling Mrs. McCathery that he was not
so very wet, that he was glad he had been of some help.

Liam's breath stopped. The voice was Colin's.

Careful to make no sound at all, Liam shoved the letters back into the hatbox and the hatbox into the armoire. On the wall, Mr. McCartney's watch ticked and ticked and ticked while Mr. McCathery stared out from his picture frame, his expression solemn, as if he knew he were, in fact, a dead man and locked up in this frame forever and ever.

Liam was as still as Mr. McCathery. But somehow he must make a move, he told himself. He must escape.

CHAPTER EIGHT

INSIDE THE DOOR TO THE GARRET ROOMS, Liam called out for Alice Ann, but no one was there. Glad that she'd gone out, he pulled off his muddied boots. His breath came fast because he had charged up the stairs and because the fear he felt when trapped inside Mrs. McCathery's room was still in him. It stayed in him the way cold might on a wintry day, even when he stood by the roaring hearth in Lord Clapham's kitchen.

Read, he told himself. *There's no time to be afraid. Read.* He crossed to the casement windows, where the light was best. Just then he heard pounding steps on the stairs. It was Colin, who threw the door open and said sharply, "What were you doing just now?"

Liam turned to face him. "What do you mean?"

"Downstairs, in Mrs. McCathery's flat, what were you after?"

"Why should I be in her flat?"

Colin slammed the door behind him. "So why were

you coming out of her window then?" Crossing to where Liam stood, he spoke as slowly and deliberately as a judge. "I am standing at the kitchen window. She had me shut it, with the rain getting in, and I saw you climbing out another window."

"I don't know what you are talking about."

"I saw you! And look at how wet you are, and the mud on you, so don't be denying it. A liar you are, and a thief besides." Colin's hands were searching Liam's pockets. They pulled at his waistband. "What have you got there?"

Liam's mouth went dry as Colin pulled the letters out and slipped one from its envelope. "Why would you be after bothering with Mrs. McCathery's letters?" he asked. "Sure you have no business with letters of hers." He shook the letter out, eyes now turning from Liam's face to what was in his hand.

What had his father done? What would Colin read?

Liam grabbed at the paper. Colin jerked it away, saying, "They are none of yours, Liam Tanner."

Liam butted at him, and, in response, Colin raised a hard knee to Liam's stomach. Suddenly Liam had no breath in his body, only pain. Suddenly Colin seemed taller than ever. He grinned and held the letters up, far above Liam's head.

"You want this and the others?" he asked. "If you want these letters, why you can have them."

"Give them to me then."

"You do what I say, and I will hand them straight over to you."

"Do what?" Liam asked.

"Soon enough you will find out. Just come with me."

"Where?"

"This morning, while you were sneaking about in Mrs. McCathery's apartment," Colin said, "I was putting up posters—for a talk my father and your uncle are giving on Saturday night. I went up and down these streets, and I found a thing or two that might prove of interest to us. Now will you be doing what I say or asking questions the livelong day?"

Liam guessed this was a trap but knew there was no way he could get the letters out of Colin's hands if they stayed in this room.

At the door Liam picked up his boots. In the right one was the hole Colin had made on the ship. The cardboard that covered it from the inside was muddy and soaked with rain. He felt the fury he had felt for Colin when he had first found that sole torn, a nail holding it to a plank.

A question burst out of his mouth. "Whose boots were these then if they were not yours?" He looked up, in time to see the single second of panic in Colin's eyes. "Whose? Tell me."

"Fergus's."

"And who is Fergus?"

"My brother." Colin spat his answer out. "Those were his boots."

"I never heard anyone speak of a Fergus."

"Nobody does speak of him. That is a fact."

There must have been some disgrace if nobody spoke of this brother. That was why Uncle Patrick had ordered him to be silent on the matter of the boots.

"What did he do then, that nobody will speak of this fine brother of yours?"

"That is not a thing that concerns you." Liam saw Colin draw back as he spoke and saw his body tense, a flash of loathing in his eyes. In that moment he thought that Colin meant to kick him. It was the look he had—of taking a measure, as if about to kick a rock or a ball. But Colin didn't kick out. He looked toward the two garret windows for a moment, a peculiar, blank expression in his eyes. Then he stared at Liam again. "Test your courage I will this day," he said. "We will see what stuff you are made of. And for every deed you perform, you will have a letter back."

"You give me your word? Is your word worth anything at all?"

"You will see I keep my word, once it is given."

Even though he hated Colin, Liam believed him. Even though he was supposed to look for a job, he would go with him and do whatever Colin wanted. By tonight, he would know about his father. He might not have work, but he would give his uncle some excuse.

By the railroad tracks on Eleventh Avenue, two small boys picked up stray pieces of coal. They resembled each other, with shaggy black hair and sharp little faces, and Liam took them for brothers. The younger boy wore a ragged jacket. The older boy had on a shiny black vest.

When Colin and Liam approached, the younger one held his pail in front of him with both hands and said, "Don't belong to the railroad, this here coal. Fell off them cars the railroad got. Ain't none of theirs, not no

more." Suspiciously, he added, "Ain't none of yours neither." On his face was a sour expression. He looked like
a tiny old man.

Colin ignored him and said to Liam, "I walked all the
way over to this river early this morning. I saw a train
come through. We'll wait for the next one, you and me."

"Why?" Liam asked.

Colin didn't answer his question. Liam didn't ask again.
He tucked his cold hands into the sleeves of his jacket
to warm them. The boys wandered off, stepping from
one railroad tie to the next, scooping up any coal they
found. In ten minutes they wandered back. The older one
plunked his bucket down and pointed to the north. "There
he comes," he said to Colin and Liam. "See there?"

And Liam did see. A man rode toward them on a dap-
pled horse. When, after minutes more, he closed in on
them, the rider yelled, "Train coming! Train on its way!"

The older boy hooked a thumb in his vest pocket,
shifted his weight to one leg, and said, "That's the cowboy they send on ahead to warn you off the tracks. Man
got killed last week, some hobo got himself wrecked.
Why you think they call it Death Avenue, if it ain't 'cuz
folks die regular here?" He nodded at his little brother.
"Ma doesn't want him or me squished flat. Gotta stay
clear once the cowboy comes, she says."

In the distance, pressed against the tracks, was the
dark train. "Get ready," Colin said. "You will cross the
tracks when I say so."

Liam eyed the train. Minute by minute, it grew larger,
like some swelling beast. He told himself he could outrun

any other boy, and he would outrun this train. Smoke spilling from its chimney, it was roaring down the track.

Liam crouched. He dug his toes into the ground. Still Colin's signal did not come, and now each second of waiting seemed long.

"You gotta be crazy to cross over these tracks," the older boy said to Liam, a worried look on his face. "That train's a killer." He gripped his brother's shoulder and made him take a half-dozen steps backward.

Liam kept himself from looking in Colin's direction. Colin would hope he'd do that. He wanted him to beg for the signal.

Behind the engine, the long line of cars whipped from side to side, coming closer and closer. Out of the corner of his eye, Liam could see the younger boy covering his ears against the unstoppable noise of the train's wheels. Under his feet the ground began to shake. Now he sighted the engineer's beefy face and the checkered scarf tied around his neck. It was too late unless Colin—

"Go!"

At once Liam ran, arms outstretched for balance. His foot touched the track. There was blast after blast of the train's whistle and the engineer's bellowing yell and the train shadowing all there was of sun and sky. A dark night descended in one terrifying instant of time.

And then he was on the other side, leaping, and the sun was leaping, flashing across rubble and ragged grass and pebbles and sticks. Liam tripped. He sprawled out flat. Life was the breath he took and the pebbles that rubbed against his palms and the tangle of short weeds he was looking at and the sunlight.

After a moment, Liam rolled and sat up, watching the clattering string of cars that swayed behind the engine. He wiped dirt from his face and pants. He ran his hands through his bristly hair and clapped his hat back on his head.

After the last car passed, lurching down the track, the smaller of the two boys crossed over the ties. He lugged his pail of coal. "You just lucky you ain't squashed flat," he announced when he was directly in front of Liam.

"Ah, but I'm not," Liam said, grinning. The boy grinned back. A front tooth was broken in half, a baby tooth, its edge jagged.

Colin reached Liam next. Without a word, he held a letter out. Liam took it.

Liam followed Colin along Ninth Avenue. When he looked through the doorway of one building, he saw a skinny black man who sat under a gas lamp at a piano. His head was tossed back. He played so fast his fingers flew, but he didn't look once at the piano keys. His fingers knew them all by heart.

This was a new world, populated by people who came in all shades and sizes. Here no one, except Colin, would care that he was not Irish through and through.

A peddler yelled at them. He waved a wide-brimmed cap and snatched up another just like it. "You boys, here's two just the same. One for each of you!"

A thought crossed Liam's mind. Michael Lanigan was

across the sea; Ireland was, too. He and Colin could have left hate there. Instead they had pulled hate along after them the way a child pulled a toy on a string. It made no sense.

Colin was staring at a half-dozen men who turned down an alley, jostling each other, talking in excited voices. "I bet they are up to something," he said to Liam. "Let's see where they're going."

Liam followed Colin into the alley. It ended at a fence, where a heavy-set man stood in front of a wooden gate. When Colin tried to walk around him, the man said, "Private party. Only people I know come to this party, and I never seen the two of you before." His two front teeth were stained by tobacco. "Go on, get on out of here."

"What are they but kids?" a voice behind them said. Liam turned. The woman who stood there was as skinny as a rail and had a pointed nose and laughing green eyes. In a teasing voice she said to the man, "Weren't you a kid once? Didn't you want in on everything and anything back then? Me, I sure did." Then she came closer and stood right in front of the man, grinning. "Come on," she said, "you're not too old to remember what fun was like, are you?"

The man pursed his lips and looked at Colin and Liam. "All right then, but don't you two go gabbing to everybody about what goes on in there. That's all. It's not exactly legal. You'd only get yourself in trouble. And me and her, too." Then he added, "Seeing as she's a steady customer, I don't want any trouble comin' her way." He waved them on.

The woman gave them a wink. "I favor kids," she said, "kids and fun."

Liam and Colin entered a cramped yard. On one end, the yard was bordered by a shed, and at the other end, by a tumbledown two-story house. A tall fence ran all around it. In the center of the space was a ring, and in the center of the ring, a man held a white rooster. He glared at a man holding a russet one.

Grasped tightly by the men, the birds thrust their heads forward, lunging madly. They had red, furious eyes. Attached to their feet, on leather bracelets, were razor-thin blades, bright spurs that glinted in the sun.

The two men stepped back and released the birds. The russet gamecock crowed, and both birds exploded in the air. They whirled up. When the russet bird pounced, the white rooster fluttered to the side and then spun upwards, his wings battering the rooster below him, his beak ripping at its head. The blades he wore slashed at its neck. The russet rooster touched the ground and faltered. Immediately, the white rooster was on him, striking him again and again with his dagger-like metal spurs. In three minutes, it was all but over, with the russet rooster on its belly, thrashing his wings. Dust flew up. The white rooster darted down and pecked at his opponent's eye.

Liam turned away. "Watch," Colin ordered.

Liam saw the white bird's blade slash again. The russet rooster no longer stirred. Its owner scooped it up by its feet and crawled through the ropes, complaining in a language that Liam did not recognize. The second man held the white bird up. Near him, people cheered, while he massaged its head and blew into its beak.

"Why is he doing that?" Colin asked the old man who stood next to them.

In a high voice, the man answered. "Get it perked up a bit. Get it ready for another go. That bird just won me some money and he ain't finished neither. No sir!"

A bandy-legged man crossed from side to side in the ring. He pointed at two new contestants who took their places. He flapped the bills he held and told people they would be sure to win on the next fight if they'd lost on this one. "The law of averages," he called. "Take advantage of the law of averages. Why we're talking science now! You got science on your side."

A short fat man yelled out that the speckled rooster was a killer. Listening to the rising shouts, Liam remembered how, when they were on the ship, he had bragged to Mr. Gavin of Cuchullain's feats in battle and of Finn MacCool's. Mr. Gavin had talked of the chickens Liam and his uncle had killed. "And if chickens were men, what then?" he had asked.

And if chickens were men, Liam thought now, then the Hell's Kitchen yard was their battlefield, and the white rooster a victorious Cuchullain. Mr. Gavin would claim that a battle was no more glorious than this.

Colin was crossing to the other side of the yard. Without being told, Liam went with him. Behind the ring they found cages and crates that held a few dozen birds. The man with the russet rooster was there. He cursed loudly and tossed the rooster down, and then marched off, talking to himself in a fuming voice.

Colin prodded the rooster with his foot.

"Opportunities arrive. They come when you do not expect them. Here is one," he said to Liam. "Pick it up."

Liam reached down and lifted the dead rooster by its feet.

"I once heard of a man who would bite the head off a chicken," Colin said. "Live or dead, it did not matter."

Liam said, "He must have been a fine gentleman, skilled at a thing like that."

"No doubt he was, and would you do the same yourself then?"

"I would not."

Colin drew a letter out. He held it up. "Do it for me," he said. "For me and Michael Lanigan. Would Michael not like that sight? Ah, Michael would. That he would."

Liam stared at Colin's thin smile and at the letter. Then he shrugged, as if he didn't care. The neck of the chicken was in his mouth. He bit down. He clenched his eyes, bit harder, and felt a trickle of blood in his throat. When he tore at the neck with his teeth, he heard Colin's laughter. If hate had a sound, it would be that sound. If it had a taste, it would be the taste in his mouth.

Furious, Liam threw the rooster to the ground. Colin prodded it with his foot while Liam spit out blood and feathers.

"This rooster has a head yet," Colin said. "You are not finished. Pick it up."

"I won't," Liam answered.

"One letter you have. If you fail again, 'tis all you will have. I cannot give you chance after chance to win them back, now can I?

CHAPTER NINE

ONCE MORE COLIN AND LIAM crossed over the rail-road tracks. Though the boys with their coal buckets had disappeared, others were scavenging. A girl of eleven or twelve years of age shoved a crate tied to roller skates ahead of her. It was filled with junk. Colin and Liam left her and her load of cans and bottles behind. When they reached the Hudson River, they walked out on a pier that was supported by half-rotten timbers. The severed head of a pig floated in the water, snout-up, as if it were sniffing the air. For a moment Liam feared that Colin would make him fetch the stinking thing out.

He didn't. Colin only licked his lips and looked out across the water. New Jersey was there. Its sprawling, rickety structures were like the ones on their own side of the river. There were tanneries, slaughterhouses, lum-beryards, icehouses, and warehouses—all dependent on the river. From here, boats could carry goods anywhere.

They left the pier and walked south. A barge moved

slowly up the river. A steamboat with a paddlewheel sped down it. Sailboats and one-man skiffs crossed from one shore to the other. Finally they turned east. Colin led them through a market, where men were selling lamb, beef, bear meat, frogs' legs, and live pheasant. Without the driver's knowing, they jumped on a wagon. Tucked low, Liam heard the driver bellow at the buggies and hansoms that cut him off and at the children who zig-zagged in and out of traffic.

When Colin nudged him and jumped from the wagon, Liam jumped down after him. He landed inches from a girl of four or five, who retreated behind a huge girder that supported elevated tracks. In the girl's basket were small, tied bundles of radishes and mint that she was selling.

Liam had no idea where he and Colin were, but on the street, tenements stood shoulder to shoulder in a never-ending row. Nowhere was there a simple whitewashed house. Nowhere was there a front yard, a tumbledown fence, or a goat or pig, like in Hell's Kitchen. Above the tenements, the sky was nothing more than a thin strip of blue, as if a scissors had snipped away the rest of it. Liam wondered if the scampering children could even imagine the huge sky that stretched over Ireland.

On a patch of sidewalk, a child was drawing a hopscotch court in chalk. At the corner, an organ grinder's monkey accepted a penny from a toddling girl. At the corner after that, a man lowered a basket from a fifth-floor window. A peddler grabbed money out of it and put oysters in. After he gave a shout, his customer pulled the basket up.

Colin hardly looked at what was going on. He

marched on and on. He acted as if he knew exactly where he was going. But how could he? And how would they find their way home again?

They had come to a park, where children crowded close to cages that held chickens and rabbits. They left the park. Colin was studying the people around them. "Her," he said abruptly, pointing to a girl who stood on a stoop a few yards away. "You will take her purse."

"I do not want her purse."

"You will do what I tell you to do."

"Didn't you call me a thief this morning, for taking Mrs. McCathery's letters? Now who is the thief?"

"You will bring the purse to me, and I will give it back to the girl, and she will thank me for it, and that is how this story will end, without thievery at all. Now will you be getting into an unholy dither or doing what I say?"

Colin looked as stern as a preacher, which made Liam want to laugh when he thought of what Colin was asking him to do. But now Colin was pointing to a huge gold-colored tooth that hung outside a building on the street that intersected the one they were on. "'Tis a dentist's office. It's there we'll meet, a block from where we stand."

"I want two letters for this," Liam said.

"It is not you who makes such decisions."

The girl was approaching a peddler, who sold crushed lemon ice. He ran one hand through his long beard while reaching for her money with the other. The purse dangled loosely in her hand.

"Two letters," Liam insisted.

"Two letters then," Colin grumbled, "but if you do not succeed, there will never be another letter at all. Not one."

As soon as the words were out, Liam ran. When he snatched at the girl's purse, it was the peddler who shouted, not the girl. By then, Liam was tearing across the street. A horse that pulled a wagon startled as he flew under its nose. He leapt over the legs of a cripple who sat against a wall, a crutch in his lap. After two minutes, jacket open and shirttail flying, Liam glanced back. No one gave chase. Now, with witnesses well behind him, he would be just another boy running in the streets, not a thief.

Just as he was about to pass a woman with a basket, she stepped into his path. Frowsy hair tumbled into her eyes. "Walk, why don't you, idiot boy! You'll be knocking people over!" She struck at his chest with her fist. Liam circled around her. He took a deep breath that filled his lungs. Just ahead was a corner. He would turn there and make his way back to the spot where he and Colin were supposed to meet, under the large gold tooth at the dentist's office. He took another breath and felt his racing heart decelerate.

Where did the hand come from? He turned, and there was the girl who owned the purse, with her flying hair and her reddened cheeks and angry eyes. How had she caught up with him? How fast could a girl run? She clutched at his shirt. With all his might Liam dived forward. Suddenly, instead of pulling, she pushed, throwing her whole body at him. Down he went.

Like a demon, the girl leapt on Liam, pulling at the purse now, shouting out. He could not understand the words. He didn't know what language she was using, but he answered in Gaelic, for all day he had been speaking it with Colin. He was telling her she was to have had the purse back. It was a trick, and nothing more. He didn't care about her money. But she only grabbed at his hair. People were gathering around them. A woman was shrieking. A man struck him on the back, and then raised his arm to strike again.

He *must* get away. Teeth clamping viciously, he bit at the girl's hand. She gave a cry and he twisted, trying to scramble up. She pinned his arms. When she bounced on his stomach, once and again and again, pain shot up in the place where Colin had kneed him back in the garret room. Then hands were seizing Liam. He was caught.

"What good will it do, you saying nothing at all? Now tell me who you are." The policeman's buttoned uniform was stretched to the breaking point across his broad chest. "Not a word out of you, huh? You're some little greenhorn is what I think. Can't talk English, is that it? Fresh off the boat, is that who you are? And stupid as they come, and doesn't he stink besides?"

This last question was addressed to a desk sergeant, who paid them no mind. "How about we ship him off in the Black Maria, down to the Tombs?" Still the desk sergeant did not take any part in this one-sided conversation. He didn't even look up.

"The Tombs, we got big tubs of water down there, throw you in one with thirty or forty of 'em at once is how we do it. That's how we get rid of the stink." Still

Liam did not say a word. He had not spoken since the crowd had surrounded him. He had said nothing when one bull-necked man slapped him about. He had said nothing to the man who dragged him to this police station by the collar of his coat.

When the policeman rifled through Liam's pockets, he took the blue-gray stone from Mum's grave. Liam wanted to grab it back. He took a piece of twine, three bottle caps, and a baseball card Liam had found. From Liam's other pocket, he fished out the letter that Liam had won back from Colin. He threw everything down in front of the desk sergeant, who pushed it all aside.

Colin still had the other letters. Would he read them?

"You hear me? Come along! I don't like repeating myself." Thinking about Colin, Liam hadn't heard him. "We got a holding pen below that will fit you like a shoe, that it will." That was said with a cuff to the back of Liam's head, and then Liam was led down uneven stone stairs and into a corridor.

On a shelf, a kerosene light sputtered. So did the policeman's moving shadow. Someone yelled out that he needed medicine, that his cough would be the death of him. The officer ignored the shout. He opened a barred door to a cell. Inside, one man sat cross-legged on a narrow bench. "We got company, looks like," he announced.

When the policeman pushed Liam inside, Liam realized that a second man was squatting in a corner. There was something crazy in the way this man cocked his head from side to side. He roosted there like a broody hen setting on eggs.

"Hey," the policeman called. "You'll want this." He tossed a gray blanket at Liam's head. "He don't talk none," the policeman added, speaking to the two prisoners.

The door clanked shut. The key turned in its lock. Both men examined him. Liam wished he could hide. Nervous, he tucked his hands inside the blanket. The man who sat cross-legged on the bench pointed a finger at him. "He says you don't talk. And this other one don't neither, unless it's when he's dreaming. All night long, you'll see, you're trying to get shut-eye, and he is mumbling away, talking in his sleep, and nothing I do stops him."

There was a pail by Liam's leg, which seemed to be filled with water. He wanted to ask if it was put there for drinking, but he decided he wouldn't utter a single word. Let everyone think he could not speak. It was the only way, he told himself. His uncle must not find out that he was here. Colin must not. Mr. Gavin and Mrs. McCathery must not. Somehow he would get out of here without anyone knowing where he had been.

Liam leaned against the bars and shoved his hands into his pockets. They were empty. The letter that he had slipped into the right one was upstairs now, among a hundred other papers scattered carelessly about the sergeant's desk. Would he ever see it again? Had he lost it for good, along with all the clues that it contained?

Alice Ann had told him that their father had left Lord Clapham's estate in a horse-drawn wagon, his head buried in his hands. With the letter snatched away, it felt as if his father were disappearing a second time. He, not

Alice Ann, was the one running desperately this time, trying to keep his father in sight.

From the other side of the cell wall came short spurts of tapping. It sounded like a person was trying to signal to the men on this side of the wall, but neither looked up. After a time, the tapping stopped. The man on the bench began to snore. Outside, night would be falling. The flame in the hall's kerosene lamp quivered. The lamp burned night and day, Liam guessed. Inside this closed cell, day and night would always be the same.

In the middle of the night a sharp, rattling noise woke Liam from a doze. At first, not remembering where he was, he sat straight up, terrified. The rattle stopped. It was only someone dragging a tin plate across the floor of his cell, or a belt buckle, Liam decided. It was nothing.

Eyes wide open, he lay on his back, unable to sleep. He thought of Fiona, his girlfriend in Kildare, wishing he could talk to her right now. She always listened when he told her about some fix he was in. She always seemed to understand what had happened. He remembered how she would lean toward him, watching him with all her might.

Fiona was nowhere near now.

Liam brushed off a cockroach that crawled along the calf of his leg. Hoping the two men in his cell were asleep, he got up to use a night bucket that was tucked in the furthest corner. Afterward, he settled himself down again, wrapping the gray blanket around him as tightly as he could, like a shield.

Somehow the night passed. The day began with the

shouts of the jailed men and the clanking of doors that were opened so that food could be passed into the cells. A man poured coffee into tin mugs that he set near the bars. Liam saw hands snake out to grab them.

The day was even longer than the night had been. In Liam's cell, the man who had squatted like a broody hen over its eggs the day before continued to do that. The second man sat on his bench. Today he had a pack of cards. Time and again he laid the cards out in rows, playing solitaire, occasionally saying something to Liam, not seeming to care that Liam didn't answer.

In the evening, the broody-hen man lay down. He began to mutter to himself in a singsong. Just then there was a banging of feet on the stairway. There were voices. One was Mrs. McCathery's. The sound brought Liam to his feet. Quickly, he brushed his hair back. He straightened his shirt.

In the gloom of the hallway, from the other side of the bars, Mrs. McCathery faced him. The policeman at her side jangled his keys. She was as tall as he was and as grim, and she was saying, "Heavens above, just look at you."

The policeman led the way as they climbed the stairs, and the desk sergeant laid out items that had been taken from Liam the day before—the twine and the bottle caps, the baseball card and Mum's blue-gray stone.

There was no letter.

"Come along," Mrs. McCathery said when he stood there, hesitating.

He couldn't ask for the letter in front of her. He scooped up his belongings.

Then Liam was in Mr. Hapwood's wagon, the horse called Delmonico pulling it through the nighttime streets. A light rain fell. At first no one spoke, not Mr. Hapwood on Liam's left, not Mrs. McCathery on his right, and not Liam, wedged in between them. The wagon made the only noise, its metal wheels grating on the brick surface of the street. After they turned onto Broadway, where granite blocks covered the cobblestones, the clatter diminished.

Finally, Mr. Hapwood said, "Well, you arrived on these shores only Monday. Then, come Wednesday, just yesterday, you got yourself locked up. That takes some doing, getting into jail quick as you did from off the boat. Not many do it that quick." He laughed.

Mrs. McCathery said, "Lord have mercy, whatever was it that prompted you to rob that girl? Whyever did you do it, Liam?"

He wanted to tell her of Colin's part. He wanted to tell her—or someone—of how he had barreled across the tracks ahead of the train and put the rooster's disgusting, bloody head in his mouth and how the jail cell walls were damp and the floor hard and how he hated Colin for it all. He said nothing, and she said, "A policeman came banging on my door, putting on grand airs, as if I were the one who had committed a crime."

Liam dropped his gaze and studied his own wriggling, nervous fingers, wondering how the police had found her.

"For all that," Mrs. McCathery went on, "the girl did not press charges, and that has saved your skin. Once she got her purse, she just went about her own business, it seems. Still, a goodly wait you would have had, if I hadn't come. And they could have sent you to the Tombs. They have a boy's prison there, with no lack of customers, you can be sure. And you'd find maggots in the soup they serve. It's what you could have supped on tonight, if the police hadn't found my letter in your pocket, the address on it plain as can be, plain as the nose on your face. They came to fetch me."

That's how they had found Mrs. McCathery, and that's why the letter was not returned to him with his other things.

Abruptly Mrs. McCathery twisted away. It seemed that she could not bear the sight of him.

In the same moment Mr. Hapwood turned to have a look for himself. He was like a one-eyed Cyclops, the lid of his left eye drooping low and in the right a gleam of amusement. "They hang someone down there, in those Tombs, don't all the folks come around," he said. "It's a regular spectacle."

"Up to the top floors in buildings across the street they go," Mrs. McCathery agreed, "scores of people do, to have a peep over the walls at the ghastly goings-ons."

The rain was falling more steadily now. Drops fell from Liam's cap to his neck. Mrs. McCathery raised a black umbrella and said in an angry mutter, "You had no right to that girl's purse—to her poor wages."

He could not explain.

While Delmonico plodded along, Liam stared out at Broadway's electric lights. In their white glare, drops of rain seemed to line themselves into whip-thin filaments.

In the glare he could read the sign fastened, front and back, across a scrawny man's shoulders: *Do You Love Your Baby? Then Give It Moggs' Mixture.*

Mrs. McCathery's biting voice came again. "And why did you have my letter? How did it come to be in your pocket?"

Slowly Liam confessed. "I took it from your bedroom. I wanted to read what Mum wrote about my father. I'm sorry."

"Sorry, to be sure." Saying that, Mrs. McCathery snapped open the reticule that sat in her lap. His mother's letter lay on top, crumpled now. Mrs. McCathery smoothed it before snapping the reticule's clasp closed. "I cannot see how you would be anything but sorry, knowing what you now do about your father and the great disgrace he brought down on your mother's head."

At the words, Liam's own head came up. Mrs. McCathery thought that he had read that letter. Could he make her say more? "The letter has not made me happier," he answered quickly. "I can't understand what my father did." Eyes on the street, Mrs. McCathery did not see Liam's expression, like that of a dog that was begging for a bone. He prompted her a second time. "I cannot understand it at all."

"It passes anyone's understanding," she replied. "Yet your father loved her. That is a thing Molly never doubted. She once told me that William might bring her a cup of tea, singing a bit of a song to her. And when children came, you and your sister, he was overjoyed, she said. *Overjoyed,* that is the very word she used. He always loved the two of you. All that is no excuse, of course, for what he did. In the end wasn't it his true wife's brother who found William out? Across the Irish Sea the brother came, as soon as he discovered that William had married again and where William had gone. He went straight from London to Lord Clapham's grand house. In a positive fury he was."

Mrs. McCathery straightened a glove, pulling at the leather. "And what was your mother to do, knowing of another wife left behind in England with three children of her own, knowing that her marriage was no marriage at all? All the priests on God's Earth would say the same to be sure. And if William Tanner brought disgrace down upon your mother's head, why he disgraced his children, too. Of course, she never wanted you and Alice Ann to know of it."

Words spun in Liam's brain—*Another wife . . . three children . . . a marriage that was not a marriage at all . . .*

Mr. Hapwood's wagon passed a girl who was half Liam's size. Liam heard her singsong, "Buy your hot corn, lily-white and smoking hot, smoking hot, just from the pot." The girl's eyes followed one passer-by, and then darted to the next. She stood under a streetlamp, its light washing across her wet face. She was like some gleaming figure in a dream.

Mr. Hapwood shook the reins and said, "Truth is, I'm not all that surprised this one got into trouble. From the start, he reminded me of one of them no-good boys that chased me down, one just his size. He got those same pale blue eyes, those straight eyebrows, the same nose. I swear this here Liam could be him."

"Liam was across an entire ocean at the time. He wasn't one of those who came after you!"

"From time to time, I see somebody that looks like one of them, why it all just rises up in my gullet. I feel the need to spit it back out, I swear."

Who had gone after Mr. Hapwood?

"Leave Liam be, Ezekiel. Though I am hardly in the mood to defend him from you or anybody else tonight," Mrs. McCathery said, before falling silent for good. For blocks and blocks not a word was spoken. The two seemed for now to have forgotten about him. That was just as well, Liam told himself.

Yet, ignored entirely, he was lonely. His loneliness seemed to take a shape—it was the same shape as their squabbling and his own father's great lie and the dark night and the chill wind and the hunger in his belly and Mrs. McCathery's hat, which drooped in the rain.

CHAPTER TEN

BEFORE GOING TO FETCH LIAM at the Eldridge Street station, Mrs. McCathery had knocked on Uncle Patrick's door. He wasn't home because he was out looking for Liam. Returning now with Liam, Mrs. McCathery knocked again. This time the door opened. Uncle Patrick stood in front of them. Words burst out of his mouth— "Gone a night and a day! No sign of you, no word of any kind, and myself chasing about the streets after you!"

As they stepped inside, Alice Ann rose up from a chair, holding the sock she had been darning. "I thought you were lost or run over, Liam. I was worried sick. I went looking for you. I lit a candle for you in the church and prayed to St. Jude. Liam, where were you?"

Into the long silence came Mrs. McCathery's voice. "I don't have the words, Liam. It's you must do the telling."

"The telling, what telling is there?" Uncle Patrick demanded. "You were to be looking for work yesterday, but you disappeared off the face of the Earth!"

Liam sidled to the wall. Beside his head was a picture Alice Ann had pinned up of an Irish maid who rested a hand on an ivy-entwined harp. He was as quiet as the maid was.

"Liam?" Alice Ann prompted.

Liam's wet coat felt like a great weight, pressing him down. "In jail. They took me into a jail. I took a girl's purse. I was going to give it back. It was only a trick, but she . . . "

Uncle Patrick was on top of him before he could finish the sentence. With his open hand, he slapped Liam about the head. Liam twisted away. "Stay still! None of that. 'Tis the strap then, boyo, if you will go ducking away from me!" He stomped off. In seconds, he returned, carrying the same black strap that had dangled from the cabin wall in Ireland.

What kind of man would carry such a thing across the ocean so he could beat a boy if the need arose?

Then Uncle Patrick pushed his face against the wall and hit Liam across his thighs with such force that Liam felt his knees buckle under him. When he walloped Liam again, Liam heard Alice Ann cry, "Uncle! Uncle, please!"

"You, too, missy, if you try to interfere."

At Alice Ann's screech, Liam jerked around, in time to see the strap slice at his sister's chest. Her eyes were frightened, then surprised, and then angry. Her chin came up. Never had anyone hit his sister, Liam knew. Never. She was the obedient one, the smiling one. But now she was like a person he had never met. Scowling, teeth bared, she grabbed at the leather. She yanked with all her might, and the strap slipped out of Uncle Patrick's hands.

Alice Ann faced him, furious. "Mother never hit us, unless it was a slap on our behinds. Not once was there a cane or a strap or a stick."

Just as Uncle Patrick lunged for the strap, Mrs. McCathery stepped in front of him. In a commanding voice, she said, "Molly left them in your care, Patrick! You are her brother, and kin to them."

Uncle Patrick's arms went limp. Mrs. McCathery touched his arm and said more quietly, "And don't I remember how it was Molly who met you on the dock at Cleegan when you rowed in with a catch of mackerel, when a whole fleet came in together. Nine or ten years of age she was, no more than that, but she would count out the fish for you. She would set a fish to the side for every hundred she counted, so she could keep her sums straight. I was there. I saw her doing that, and her only a little mite of a thing."

Liam had never seen the expression that was on his uncle's face. He seemed another man for a moment, someone kind and harmless. "Aye," he answered, "and wasn't it Molly herself trailing behind me like a puppy when the turf was cut, wanting to help me."

It seemed he had fallen under a spell. If there were a spell, Liam decided, Mum had cast it from the heavens. He slipped his hand deep into his trouser pocket and around the stone from his mother's grave, wishing her into this room.

And then Mum came into his mind and seemed so

real, she was almost alive again. She was standing on the back steps off the kitchen, a maid's white apron covering her dark skirt, her dark curls tucked up into a maid's white cap. Smiling, she asked, "Where are you off to?" and he answered, "Up Clysdale Hill, for a walk."

"Ah, it's a gorgeous day for that," she said, "but you will have to hurry if you are to be home before dark." At the fence, when he turned, she waved with one hand. With the other, she shielded her eyes from the sun. She seemed to be saluting him.

The memory, sharp as a picture in its frame, faded away, but he remembered when he had seen Mum like this. It was less than a year ago. He had been on his way to meet Fiona. That afternoon they had taken the narrow trail that wound around and around Clysdale Hill like a ribbon, all the way to the top. They walked fast. Though short of breath, Fiona kept talking, telling him about a Dr. Jekyll and a Mr. Hyde. She knew how to read, and she had been reading the tale in a book the night before. Dr. Jekyll and Mr. Hyde were two men in one, she claimed, a reasonable man but a killer too. *Dual nature*, she had called it, clinging to Liam's hand, devil and good come together in one being.

Mrs. McCathery took the strap from Alice Ann and handed it to Uncle Patrick. He drew it across the palm of his left hand, stroking it with bent fingers. His uncle was two men in one. Uncle Patrick had loved his own sister once, and then hated her and her children. He was a kind man, and at the same time he was a hard man who liked that strap and who scowled at Liam.

"But what of him?" he asked. "What do we do with that boy there?"

Mrs. McCathery replied, "You said he was to have a job, and the sooner the better, you said. I spoke tonight with Mr. Hapwood, and he has agreed to take Liam on. Liam can go out with him on the wagon to make deliveries tomorrow morning, if you like. He can help in the stable. There's plenty of work for him, and Mr. Hapwood is willing to keep a close eye on him."

Uncle Patrick frowned and said, "But he is a black man, Mr. Hapwood is."

"And what harm is there in that? Why, he's young and energetic. He's smarter than any other man you'd find on these streets. In the end, won't he make something of himself? Mr. Hapwood has a future ahead of him. Take my word on that. Liam could not do better."

When Uncle Patrick did not reply, Mrs. McCathery asked, "And haven't you ever seen a black person before?"

Liam knew that there was not one black in all of Connemara. Maybe there was not a black in all of Ireland. Africans had never been carried off to Ireland in chains, the way they had been carried here. Unless enslaved, unless forced, why would they ever settle in wet, windy Ireland, a land completely different from their own hot Africa?

Uncle Patrick fingered the strap. "I'll not have it," he insisted.

"Not have it? Because he is black? And did you not know, Patrick, that the very chimps in this city's zoo are given Irish names? And in the papers, in their cartoons, they make apes of us, the blacks and the Irish both. Apes—and it is such terrible nonsense!"

She added, in a voice gone quiet, "Didn't God make every race?"

Back and forth Uncle Patrick's hand went along the black strap. "Is it not myself that is in charge of the boy, set in charge by his own mother? 'Tis my business then," he scolded, "and none of yours, and there's an end to the matter. He'll not labor for your Mr. Hapwood."

A kerosene light set on the table shone up into Mrs. McCathery's face. It illuminated the red patches on her skin and the rebellious lines across her brow. Her hair had slipped from the hairpins that held it in place. Her voice, when she spoke, was uneven, as if it had come unpinned, too. "An end to the matter? But it is no small matter, is it, Patrick? These are Molly's children, and it is Molly's very life going on in them, whatever happens to them."

Saying that, she put an arm about Alice Ann's waist. Alice Ann leaned her head on Mrs. McCathery's shoulder. Their dark hair intermingled, as if it fell from one head.

Liam imagined Mrs. McCathery might put out a hand to him. She did not even glance his way. Like Alice Ann, she thought he was a thief. Mum had sent them to Mrs. McCathery. If she turned her back on him now, what would happen?

After Uncle Patrick fell asleep, Liam left their room. Quietly, he closed the door behind him and stole to the spot by the kitchen stove where Alice Ann lay on her mat. When he whispered her name, Alice Ann startled awake. Liam told her what he had learned from Mrs. McCathery—that their father had another wife and other children.

His sister put a hand to her mouth. She took it away and asked, "You're saying that he was already married when he married Mum?"

"He was."

"How could he do that to Mum? How could he?"

"But Mrs. McCathery said he loved Mum and was glad when we were born."

Alice Ann said, "He lied to Mum from the start, and she believed him. And why wouldn't she, of course? Why would she ever think he was lying?"

"I remember riding on his shoulders once," Liam murmured. "There was a field with horses, and it must have been morning. There was just a little bit of sunlight. There was morning fog." It had swirled about, as if someone was gently stirring it.

Liam's voice trailed off. Again his mind drifted to thoughts of Dr. Jekyll and Mr. Hyde, of two men in one. His father's lies were monstrous. But he loved Mum. And he had carried him on his shoulders that morning, past the horses that shied away at their approach, because he wanted to show that world to his son. Was he a monster or not?

Liam listened, as if listening for an answer, to a wind that was whistling past. It rattled the garret windows. The room's walls creaked, old as they were. Outside the scraggly bushes and thin trees would be bending this way and that. There would be cats that scuttled for cover.

There was no answer in the wind. Alice Ann was crying softly. He touched her shoulder.

The next afternoon Liam went to see Mrs. McCathery. She let Liam in. In her kitchen, a large tin clothes boiler sat on the stove. She wrung a wet skirt in the mangle and hung it on a line that was strung from one corner of the room to the other. "Sit yourself down if you like, but I've work to attend to here. Friday is my wash day." She turned to the clothes boiler. With a wooden stick, she stirred clothes, like a soup. He remembered how she had stirred the sizzling bacon in a pan for him only three days ago. Today, there was no welcoming glance.

"I've an interview today, for work," Liam announced to her.

Her head turned.

"At the pharmacy. Alice Ann went there this morning, and Mr. O'Donnell hired her straight away and mentioned that he needed a delivery boy. She ran back home and told me to come and talk to him."

"The sooner you are employed, the better." Mrs. McCathery was frowning at the rising steam, not at him, Liam told himself, but there was nothing kind about Mrs. McCathery today.

Mr. O'Donnell took off the tiny glasses he wore and polished the lenses with a clean handkerchief. "These are special glasses," he said to Liam, a proud note in his voice. "Bifocals. Ben Franklin's own invention!"

He put them back on. "Well, I hired your sister today. She put in a good word for you, and she certainly appears to be efficient and orderly. Do you take after her yourself, my boy?"

"I hope so, sir." But hope would never make him efficient and orderly, Liam knew. He added, "I'm not afraid of hard work, sir. And if it's a delivery boy you want, why I'm fast on my feet."

Mr. O'Donnell took a watch from his vest pocket and looked at the tiny hands. "A good answer, good enough, I think. You're fourteen, you say?"

"Yes, sir."

"You're working age then. There'd be no trouble with the working papers. Is that right?"

"Yes, sir."

"Six days a week, with Sundays off is what this job would entail. You would arrive every morning at seven-thirty. Does that suit you?"

"Yes, sir."

The handkerchief was out again. Mr. O'Donnell was wiping his hands with it and saying, "First thing in the morning, before any customer steps through the door, you'll sweep the shop from top to bottom. We open at eight. After that, there will be deliveries throughout the day."

He had taken a tray out. "While your sister wraps the packages and waits on customers, you'll take charge of deliveries. And you'll do whatever else needs doing—

fetching coal or going to the chemists for things I need or washing the windows." He raised his head. "This and that! That's what the job is. Is that good enough for you?"

"Yes, sir," Liam answered.

"Fine, fine."

As if those words were her cue, Alice Ann came out of the back room. She carried two packages, neatly wrapped and tied with string, and gave them to two customers, who took them and stepped out of the store. Alice Ann looked at Liam, eyebrows raised in a question.

It was then Mr. O'Donnell spoke. "We'll give you a trial run. That's settled then. Come in tomorrow. You'll go about with the boy who is quitting, Jimmy. Jimmy can show you the ropes, and you can start the job Monday."

When Liam glanced at Alice Ann, she beamed at him and then disappeared through the swinging doors and into the back once more.

On Mr. O'Donnell's tray were delicate glass bottles. One by one he held them up to the light, inspecting them, before gently putting them on the tray again. Behind him on shelves were more glass bottles, filled with mysterious liquids. There were dozens of jars, filled with mysterious powders. Ranged on the glistening counter were pestles, mortars, beakers, measuring spoons, and a scale. There was not a speck of dust anywhere, certainly not on Mr. O'Donnell, whose face glistened under the light as he ogled his bottles. A little smile played on his mouth.

Here was a meticulous man, happy in his meticulous world, believing Liam would be happy in it because he'd just said he would.

Late that afternoon, Liam followed three boys who lived in the building up to the roof, where they kept racing pigeons in coops. One was the boy named Jacob, who had seen Colin going after Liam on the stairs four days ago. And just four minutes ago, when he had seen Liam on the garret landing, he had asked if Liam wanted to see the pigeons. Liam had never met the two others, who were arguing about which pigeon was fastest.

Far below him, Liam spied the vagrant, who had threatened him on Tuesday when he went to Mr. Hapwood's stable for furnishings. He sat cross-legged in front of his tent. Liam saw Mr. Hapwood emerging from the stable, too, with the wild gray horse Liam had seen that day. Mr. Hapwood led him into a corral, a make-shift thing made of whitewashed ropes that were strung between raggedy posts. Inside that corral, he walked the horse in circles before snapping a long line onto his halter and stepping away.

Jacob took a place beside Liam, watching, too. He said, "Mr. Hapwood bought that horse for just about nothing at all because the folks who had him before were wanting to get rid of him in a hurry. He's named Dudley. Mr. Hapwood wants to make a race horse out of him."

In Mr. Hapwood's hand was a whip, its shaft six or eight feet long. When he flicked it at the horse's hocks and called out, Dudley began to trot. Around and around he went. As Mr. Hapwood fed out more line, the distance between him and the animal steadily grew.

"Just before he came here, that horse pinned a stable boy against a wall," Jacob was saying. "Once he had him pinned, he lit into him, trampled him, and almost killed him. Crippled him for good. And before that, he broke a man's leg. And before that, he bit a child's arm, just about bit it off. Mr. Hapwood got him for less than two hundred dollars, Papa heard. Papa says that was too high a price to pay. Ten dollars would be too high a price, he says, even if that thing is a thoroughbred."

"The way he moves, he's worth something," Liam answered.

"You know about horses?"

Liam nodded. Beside them, a boy had taken a pigeon out of a coop. He was talking of racing it against a neighbor's pigeon, a boy who belonged to another racing club.

Liam saw the vagrant get to his feet. Jacob said, "That man down there is crazier than a coot, and meaner than anything, and he's always after Mr. Hapwood. Watch. He'll go after him now."

"Why does he go after him?"

Jacob shrugged. "People don't always need a reason." A wide grin was on his face. "That boy on the stairs, why was he going after you?"

"Colin?"

"If that's his name. Why did he go after you? Who is he?"

"He came here from Ireland with his father, my uncle's friend," Liam answered. "In Ireland, people take sides. Colin's on one side. He thinks I'm on the other. I don't know why he thinks that. He doesn't know me."

None of the boys knew him. They didn't know that Mum had sent her children to Connemara because she was Irish and she loved it there. They didn't know how Mum had died in the candle's flickering light or how he and Alice Ann had watched, terrified. "Colin doesn't know anything at all," Liam said irritably. "Colin just wants a fight."

And Colin still had Mum's letters, Liam knew. Though he hadn't seen Colin yesterday, his first day out of the jail cell, Colin would appear soon enough. Liam was sure that he would, and that he'd be looking for a fight. He was like the vagrant who staggered towards Mr. Hapwood in the stable yard now, waving a fist.

Mr. Hapwood was drawing the gray horse closer to him. The horse stared at the vagrant and reared up. He pawed at the air with his long legs, ready to attack, it seemed. At once, the vagrant staggered backwards, retreating. Ten minutes later, Mr. Hapwood left the corral. At his side, the horse was like a huge guard.

On Saturday Liam worked alongside Jimmy, a boy with a round, honest face and a giant mole on his chin, who said he'd found a job in A. T. Stewart's Department Store. "It's a palace," he bragged, launching into a description of its wonders. "You're welcome to this old job. I'm moving up in life!" They went up yet another set of stairs. "The ones live here, they're sisters, too old to venture out much, so they get everything delivered. They hobble about, two canes each. They're regular customers."

Liam trailed after Jimmy down a dark hallway.

"You'll carry them their medicine every Saturday," Jimmy explained. "They'll want to give you a full report on every new ache, like you're the doctor. The trick is in getting away from them."

He rapped on the door. It swung open. Facing them was a little bird-like woman, a cane in each hand. She leaned forward. "Come in! Come in! We were expecting you. It's Jimmy, Sarah," she sang out as they entered.

"And Liam, Miss Mandel," Jimmy said.

Miss Mandel's sister, Sarah, joined her. "Jimmy!" she proclaimed happily.

"This here's Liam, the new boy," Jimmy told the both of them. "From now on, he's the one you want."

That night Uncle Patrick shaved and dressed carefully, and after they had had their supper, Mr. Gavin and Colin appeared, knocking at the door.

"It begins," Mr. Gavin said as they stepped inside. "Off we'll be going to the Hibernian Hall. Hundreds will be there." He looked at Alice Ann. "And your uncle and myself, we're to talk to them. There we'll be, the two of us, up on a stage, talking of Ireland and all the troubles England has brought down on her head."

Uncle Patrick was fumbling with a bow tie, a thing he never wore. "Let me help you with that thing," Mr. Gavin ordered. As he stepped in front of Uncle Patrick, Colin gripped Liam by the elbow and drew him to the windows.

"You didn't say anything?"

"About your making me steal that girl's purse? You'd know by now if I'd told anybody," Liam answered.

Colin's hair, smelling of hair oil, was plastered to his head and parted neatly down the middle. Like Uncle Patrick and Mr. Gavin, he was freshly shaved. Like them he wore a coat and vest. He looked older than he had on Wednesday, when he and Liam had tramped the streets. He looked like a man. Next to Colin, Liam felt like a boy—Mr. O'Donnell's errand boy, in charge of this and that.

"Where are my letters?" Liam asked. "I did what you asked."

"You never did bring me that girl's purse. You failed," Colin said. "Why should you have the letters?"

"Failed? When I was jailed because of you? I'm done with you then! I won't play this game."

Alice Ann was looking their way. Colin lowered his voice. "But don't I have what you want? You're not done. Not yet."

"We're ready!" Mr. Gavin called. "Come on then, Colin. You're to be a part of this tonight, lad!"

Before Colin joined them, he said softly, "And you, Liam Tanner, you're to have no part in these matters. Stay here with your sister tonight, boyo."

After the door shut, Alice Ann said, "Colin was putting up posters for the talk. They had him running about the city doing that, all day yesterday and all day today, too. He claims there are Irish judges and doctors and businessmen who can't wait to give their money to Ireland. And men who dig ditches will give, too, whatever they can."

"The money won't be his," Liam said angrily.

"No, nobody in this house will grow rich from it."

Shoes off, she massaged her stockinged feet. "Poor feet," she said, "they hurt when I stand all day."

Liam began stacking the dishes. Alice Ann said, "Mrs. McCathery says they'll ask for money for a political campaign, to give the Irish more power and more land, but she thinks that some of it will go to buying guns, too. And they are dragging Colin into it. Does he even know what he's in for?"

Liam didn't care what happened to Colin, or to the boys who called Michael Lanigan "Commandant" and who followed his orders to prove they hated the English.

"For Colin, it is like acting now, like dressing up to play a part. But one day it will be real," Alice Ann said.

"Why are you worried about Colin?"

Alice Ann waved her hand dismissively. It dropped at her side. "It's not just Colin. It's that it started so many centuries ago, all this fighting. Once it starts, it never seems to end. Why can't it stop?"

She stared at Liam, as if she really expected that he would know how to end the centuries-old battles. When he didn't answer, Alice Ann said, "I wish the fighting had never begun." She stood, picked up the kettle from the stove, and poured hot water into the dish basin. Steam erupted. Alice Ann stirred the water about with a ladle, and the steam crept higher. In that swirling mist, she was like a sibyl, issuing a prophecy, delivering a warning—"Stay clear of them, Liam. Don't let them drag you into it."

Colin had already caught him, he wanted to tell her, but he only slipped the plates and spoons and cups into her basin and kept quiet.

CHAPTER ELEVEN

ON MONDAY, in Mr. O'Donnell's pharmacy, Liam heard the tinkling of the bell that was attached to the door. He felt the rush of wet air from the street. He welcomed it because he was sweeping the floor around the coal stove, which gave off ferocious blasts of heat.

Head tucked down, he heard a customer saying he needed something to quell the burning sensation he felt too often after eating. The voice, with its rough English accent, seemed familiar somehow. Mr. O'Donnell asked the man for more information about his discomfort.

In the end, Mr. O'Donnell said, cheerfully, "Oh, we have something that should fix you up straight away."

And would the customer want to wait while he prepared a curative? Or would he have the remedy delivered perhaps?

The customer would wait. He stepped to the side, peering into a glass case at prepackaged items Mr. O'Donnell's pharmacy sold—Bromo Seltzer, wart remover, arnica salve, castor oil, witch hazel, or other simple remedies. He tapped his fingers on the glass.

He had a long, straight back and a long neck. Suddenly an image came to Liam—of his father walking through Lord Clapham's stable, his back ramrod straight, like this man's. The man's voice just now, it had sounded like his father's voice, or what Liam could remember of it.

Behind the counter, Mr. O'Donnell bent over his mortar and pestle to crush herbs for his latest concoction. Above his head were long shelves, and on the shelves were rows of brown bottles. Liam knew they contained potions of all kinds. With vigorous strokes of the broom he moved toward those shelves, wanting to inspect the man more closely. He was certain that, looking at the man head-on, he would find a man with a pursed, fat mouth or one whose ears stuck out. The man would have pockmarked skin. There would be nothing in the face that recalled his father's half-remembered features.

Liam edged closer, still sweeping, careful to not disturb Mr. O'Donnell, who might shoo him off. Occupied, Mr. O'Donnell did not seem to notice Liam, but in an instant, the stranger looked up. His eyes were as pale as Liam's own. Liam gripped the broom and took in the man's straight nose and full lower lip, remembering what his mother said when he once complained that he could barely recollect his father. *Ah, you have but to look in a mirror to find him, Liam.*

This could be his face in a mirror, the likeness he saw.

The man was glancing away now. He showed no sign of recognizing Liam.

Mr. O'Donnell looked impatiently at Liam through his tiny bifocals. He murmured, "Don't be in the way, Liam. Can't you see I'm busy here?" Liam had no choice then but to go and sweep somewhere else.

If the blue-eyed man were his father, Liam told himself, he could not let him go. He had no plan, beyond knowing that he could not lose sight of him. Without a word to Mr. O'Donnell or to Alice Ann, who was sorting inventory in the back room, he slipped through the door when the man left. Following close behind, Liam could hear the clap of his shoes on the pavement and see his coat flap in the wind.

A dray passed, loaded with barrels and pulled by two enormous Clydesdales that plodded as steadily as elephants down the center of Ninth Avenue. Each would weigh a ton. Liam thought that the sight of such fine horses would surely make his father's head turn, but the man paid no attention.

They passed a carriage house with arched windows. Through its wide-open door, Liam saw a man shoeing a pretty golden horse. The blue-eyed man didn't look, and again Liam told himself that his father would have.

Yet there was the familiar voice, the man's eyes, as pale blue as his own, and the face that looked like his own. His mother's voice sounded inside Liam's brain— *You have only to look in a mirror.*

Liam followed the man along a fence. Behind it, great piles of junk filled a large yard from one side to the other.

Two big dogs guarded it all. One stared at the blue-eyed man through flat, yellow eyes, trailing him from its side of the fence, growling.

"Get off with you," the man shouted at it. "Go on!"

At the next corner, the man turned left onto Forty-ninth Street. He strode along it before stopping at a three-story brownstone, a clean building with shuttered windows. The man went up its steps. Liam waited for two minutes before going up those same steps. Hesitantly, he opened the glass door. Inside, he read names that were posted on cardboard tabs — Hans Kruller, Esquire; Miss Milly Bently; Miss Elizabeth Reardon; Mr. Lesley Smith. They lived in apartments here, but there was no William Tanner.

But what if his father did not live here? What if he were only visiting somebody?

From a safe distance Liam stood under the gray April sky and kept watch. An hour passed. Though it was not raining, the wind was damp, and Liam thrust his cold hands in his pockets.

By now, in the pharmacy, Mr. O'Donnell would have found out that he wasn't there. He would be asking Alice Ann if it were her brother's habit to walk out on an employer on the very first day of his hire. She would say it was not Liam's habit at all. "I had hoped reliability was a family trait," he would be saying.

When his sister made excuses, Mr. O'Donnell would grumble, "That's well and good, Miss Alice Ann, but I've no delivery boy, have I? And there are customers waiting!" Liam imagined him pulling his watch from a vest pocket. He was always looking at his watch—because it was important to know the precise time.

Mr. O'Donnell would fire him immediately, Liam knew. He had only to step through the pharmacy door.

A smart young woman emerged from the building. Was it Miss Elizabeth Reardon or Miss Milly Bentley? An old man went in and came right out again. Another hour passed. The mailman arrived, weighted down by his enormous leather bag. An ice wagon pulled up, chased by small children. Using great tongs, two men carried blocks of ice into the basement of a neighboring house.

Liam was hungry. He thought of the lunch wrapped in newspaper that he had left in Mr. O'Donnell's back room, and he thought of Alice Ann staring at it forlornly while eating hers.

And then the blue-eyed man appeared. At the bottom of the stairs, he turned back the way he had come. An idea came to Liam as he watched the man stride past. Without a moment's pause, he acted on it. Chasing after the man, he called out, "Mr. Tanner! Mr. William Tanner!" When Liam was on his heels, the man turned.

"What are you shouting about?"

"I've been sent to tell you there's an important telegram, sir! It's urgent, Mr. Tanner! It's a matter of life and death!"

The man's whole face turned into a question mark. "Tanner? My name's not Tanner."

"You are sure?"

"Am I sure? Am I sure of my own name?"

"It's urgent! Some say there's a great inheritance involved!"

"Get off!" The blue-eyed man cuffed at Liam's head. Liam dodged. "A great inheritance," the man said, "and you don't look like you have a penny in your pocket to give to a living soul!"

"You are not Mr. Tanner, sir?"

"Are you insane?"

Liam stood in place as the man walked away. Disappointment nailed him to the spot. He reminded himself that only a few days ago he had claimed he wanted no part of the father who had told great devilish lies to Mum.

The man was passing the junkyard when one of the big dogs began barking uproariously. Sticking its head out of a half-open window across the street, a small dog—someone's pet—started howling in reply.

Liam didn't dare return to the pharmacy and to Mr. O'Donnell's certain rage. He could not go home until the pharmacy closed for the day, in case Uncle Patrick returned unexpectedly and found him there. Where could he go to get out of the cold?

Liam opened one of the wide doors and stepped inside Mr. Hapwood's stable. He took in the smell of hay and oiled leather and horse. He could even smell the pigeons that flew back and forth in the rafters over his head. He looked at the tack hanging from pegs on the wall to his left. How often had he cleaned tack, wiping dust from a bridle or polishing a bit? This was his world, he thought.

The pharmacy wasn't. What did he know of potions and medicines?

And if this was his world, why couldn't he ask Mr. Hapwood to hire him? Hadn't Mrs. McCathery said Mr. Hapwood would? Then, after Mr. O'Donnell fired him, he would have a job, and he would have the money that Uncle Patrick expected to receive from him each week. Uncle Patrick didn't need to know where it came from.

Delmonico's stall was empty, but the gray horse was in his, shifting nervously from foot to foot. "It's only me," Liam said, coming closer. Dudley stuck his head over the door of the stall, his wild eyes floating up in his eye sockets. Facing Liam, he rolled his upper lip back. Liam looked at his long teeth and thought the animal would snap his hand off if he could. He would attack.

"I should have brought a carrot for you, and I will when I come again," Liam said soothingly. "You like carrots. You like apples. If Mr. Hapwood hires me, I'll brush the dust and grime off that coat of yours and walk you in the yard. You would like that."

On the animal's neck were scars and nicks. Looking more closely, Liam saw that scars ran along his flanks, too. Ears flat, he pawed at the ground furiously, making a hole in the deep bedding of straw. "There's no need for such a ruckus," Liam told him.

He might be moody and wild, but he was handsome. He had long, straight legs, an arching neck, a broad forehead, a flowing dark tail, and a full dark mane. His shoulders and hindquarters rippled with muscle.

He seemed made to run, and Liam could see why Mr. Hapwood would want to have him.

"You and I, we might be friends in the end," Liam said softly. "I'll be your friend if you let me. Horses like me. You will one day. See if you don't."

Dudley answered with a defiant snort and gnashed his teeth, while Liam told himself that in this stable he would need to be wary of this horse—if Mr. Hapwood hired him.

And, above all, he must be wary of Uncle Patrick. If he worked with Mr. Hapwood, Uncle Patrick must not find out.

"You have only to slip an envelope each week from Mr. O'Donnell's desk."

"Only?"

"It's no great thing, an envelope."

"An envelope stamped with the pharmacy's address is no great thing perhaps," Alice Ann said, "but, if I help you, I'll find myself mired deeper and deeper in your schemes, Liam. I know it."

On the landing outside their door, she stood at the sink. Water dripped from the sink's pipes onto the wooden floor beneath it, which was rotting with damp. Liam imagined the sink falling straight through the floor some day, surprising those who lived below as it tumbled onto their heads, along with plaster and dust and splintering beams.

Alice Ann scrubbed a cast iron pan she had just bought from a pawnshop near the pharmacy. "I will not be part of your lying," she declared. "Uncle Patrick said you must not work for Mr. Hapwood. Don't do it! I don't care if he said he would hire you."

"If I work for Mr. Hapwood, I'll be near horses, doing what I know how to do," Liam argued.

Alice Ann watched her hands and the bar of brown soap as she spoke. "Mr. O'Donnell was in a fury, Liam. He will never have you back."

"I don't want to work in a pharmacy!"

"Well, you won't, and you're at fault, not him. He is a fair man. He's been fair with me."

"Wasn't I certain that the customer was Father when I went after him?" Liam pleaded. "I never would have left if I didn't think that."

"Ah, your blue-eyed man—but if all you told me the other night is true, what good is Father to us, even if you find him?"

Liam didn't know how to answer Alice Ann's question. Bringing the conversation back to his request instead, he said, "I must bring money home. If I hand it to Uncle in one of the pharmacy's envelopes, sealed tight like your very own..."

"It is a lie, Liam, and what if Uncle finds you in the lie. It will go worse for you then." Alice Ann scrubbed harder, frowning.

"When he is busy all the day, from sun-up until sun-down, with barely space to breathe or think, how will he find out? He was out Saturday night to talk at that hall. He's gone off tonight to one of those meetings. We hardly see Uncle Patrick or Mr. Gavin."

"Colin went off with them tonight, too," Alice Ann said.

As she spoke Colin's name, Liam felt a ripple of anger. He would never have been jailed if Colin hadn't taken the letters and interfered. Mrs. McCathery and Uncle Patrick wouldn't have turned against him. Lost in his thoughts, Liam barely noticed that Alice Ann was still talking. He shook his head, chasing Colin out of it so he could hear her.

". . . and Mr. Gavin told me that more than two hundred people were at the Hibernian Hall on Saturday night. After Uncle Patrick gave his speech, people wouldn't stop clapping. There he is, out half the night with his politics, and digging up the streets all day," she continued. "It's no wonder that he is always exhausted."

"That's what I am telling you. He stumbles off to bed every night without a word to us. If we don't tell him, he'll never find out I was fired. He won't find out if we give him two envelopes with pay inside every week, one from you and one from me."

"I cannot," Alice Ann repeated.

Liam remembered how Uncle Patrick had wanted to beat him when he came home from jail. "There will be a beating then," he said, convinced there would be, discouraged.

His sister scrubbed so hard her knuckles turned red. She took in a breath and let it out. "Mr. Hapwood said he would hire you straight away? Is that what he told you?"

"Tomorrow I can go there."

"And he'll not say a word to Uncle Patrick?"

"He will not, not after I told him what Uncle Patrick said, that he didn't want me working for a black man."

Mr. Hapwood's mouth had curled in disdain when Liam told him that. Suddenly he had stuck out a hand. "The job is yours, and I won't tell your uncle nothin'. Shake on it," he had said, a dare in his eyes—as if Liam might fear to touch his dark skin. "Go ahead. Take this man's hand." They shook hands, the contract made.

With an old rag Alice Ann dried her pan. "Ah, Liam," she said finally, "the eternal scrapes you get into!"

Another moment passed before Liam heard what he had hoped he would hear. "I'll play my part then," Alice Ann whispered. "You will have your envelope every Friday from Mr. O'Donnell's shop. Put Mr. Hapwood's money in it and give it to Uncle. And God have mercy on the both of us if he discovers what we have done."

CHAPTER TWELVE

Wᴵᵀᴴ ᴍᵁˢᶜᵁᴸᴬᴿ, ᵀᴵᴿᴱᴸᴱˢˢ ˢᵀᴿᴼᴷᴱˢ, Mr. Hapwood wielded the shovel. "You are gonna find a pit of compost in back," he told Liam, who was helping him muck out the stalls. "That's where you pile this horse dung."

Liam lifted the handles of the handcart. He had taken one step forward when Mr. Hapwood's abrupt warning came. "You stay clear of Dudley, you hear what I'm telling you? Don't go walkin' in back of him. The devil resides in those hind legs of his."

Liam made a wide berth behind the gray horse. Dudley was tall and his chest was thick with muscle, but he was thin. Edgy, nervous horses grew thin, Liam knew. Lord Clapham would not have kept a horse like that. In an instant he would have sold Dudley off to anyone who would take him.

When Liam returned, Delmonico was tied to a post in the middle of the stable, and Mr. Hapwood was sprinkling lime on the damp planks of his stall. "You ever clean the hooves on a horse before?" he asked.

"A hundred times and more I have."

"Appears you know your way around horses some."

"Where I lived in Ireland there were horses, and a special stable for the hunters, and another for the carriage horses and the ponies and the brood mares."

"A big, grand outfit, that it?"

"An earl he was, the master," Liam answered.

"An earl," Mr. Hapwood said. "Here I am brushing up against somebody gone and brushed up against an earl."

Liam felt himself tense under Mr. Hapwood's measured stare, the one eye cold, and the other all but closed.

"Delmonico don't fret none, no matter who it is goes looking at his feet. Don't got to be no earl to do it, so go on and check him good," Mr. Hapwood ordered.

His contemptuous tone was no better today than yesterday, Liam thought. Yesterday, on his first day of working for Mr. Hapwood, they had made deliveries to grocers and dry goods stores. Liam had lugged sacks of potatoes and yams and onions and heavy crates of produce. Mr. Hapwood had watched him closely the whole time, perhaps thinking that Liam would collapse before the day was out. But at day's end, Liam had forced himself to leap off the wagon the way Mr. Hapwood did, as if he weren't tired at all.

One by one, Liam picked up Delmonico's hooves so he could pry out mud and pebbles with the hoof pick Mr. Hapwood gave him. He ran his fingers over the outer hoof wall to check the shoe for loose nail ends.

The stable's black and white cat made an appearance and stood right in front of Delmonico. Even when Delmonico bent his head to nose at him, the cat didn't move away. Instead, he rubbed his back against the horse's jaw, leaning into it, enjoying a good scratch. Delmonico let the cat do that.

One horse in this stable would eat people alive, while the other would give a cat a scratch.

"You 'bout done there, boy?" It was Mr. Hapwood's raspy voice calling to him. Mr. Hapwood had slipped past Dudley and clipped a line to his halter. As he backed the horse out of his stall, Mr. Hapwood spoke steadily to him. He could be having a conversation with some other man.

Tying Dudley next to Delmonico, he said to Liam, "This here fella isn't even two years old yet. Managed to pick up a lot of bad habits in that time though. If I keep him by Delmonico pretty constant, maybe Delmonico can calm him down and teach him some manners."

Just then Delmonico nuzzled at Dudley's shoulder and nickered, and it did seem that the older horse might in fact be telling the younger one about the rules. Watching them, Mr. Hapwood said, "Delmonico is gonna settle Dudley down some. By and by, he will." There was hope in his voice. "They like company, horses do, same as you and me."

"They do," Liam agreed. He had seen a young mare left alone in a field lean against a fence, getting as close as she could to horses that were two fields away. He had seen her stare longingly in their direction, ears flicking forward and back, as if trying to hear what the other horses were saying.

Mr. Hapwood stroked the high crest of Dudley's arched neck until the horse twisted his head away, the whites of his eyes rolling back. "Arabian blood in him," he said proudly. "Thoroughbreds all got Arabian blood in their ancestry. You see it right there in that powerful neck Dudley's got."

Mr. Hapwood led Liam into Dudley's empty stall, saying, "Now you come and help me out." The old yellow dog stood up. White tufts of hair poked up around her ears. When Mr. Hapwood said, "Go on, out of our way," she stalked off on her stiff legs.

Mr. Hapwood pointed at three circular pieces of iron, which looked like discarded cogs from some machine. "This here's a cure," he said, as he tied one to a long rope. He slung the free end of the rope over a rafter, then hoisted the cog up. Mr. Hapwood gave the contraption a pull to test it. "That'll hold. Now get those other ropes and tie one on to each of these other metal things I got here." Liam did. Together they strung them alongside the first one.

"Dudley rears his hind end up and kicks like he has a mind to," Mr. Hapwood said, "he'll knock into these. It won't feel good. Not a bit. So he'll learn it's best to keep four feet on the ground at all times. A horse got bad habits? You just out-think him. Most people can't. Most people, it seems they are stupider than the horses they own. Man who had Dudley was. Paid a big price for him when he was hardly more than a suckling foal because of his bloodlines—that horse has got good blood in him. Then, after putting down a whole packet of money, what does he go and do, that fella? Mishandles him. Just about ruins him."

The raspy voice turned into a growl. "Next thing, he wants rid of Dudley." He shook his head. Mr. Hapwood was putting a coil of rope away in a cabinet, where planes, chisels, screwdrivers, and other tools were organized in neat rows. "You look at Dudley good?" he asked, glancing at Liam. "He is built like one fine horse. His daddy? Twice I seen that horse run the Coney Island track. Twice I seen him win, too. He had a way about him—sassy and fast as the dickens. Wanted nobody passing him by."

After a pause, he nodded at the gray horse and said, "Named him Dudley's Ride, after Dudley Allen."

When Liam gave him a blank look, Mr. Hapwood added, "He was a black man. Owned a horse that won the Derby and trained that horse, too." He gave Liam a challenging look, as if expecting argument.

Liam said nothing. Mr. Hapwood spoke again. "Better muck out Dudley's stall now. Throw down lime like I did in the other one. Then we'll give him a new bed to lie down in, nice and thick."

Liam raked manure and dirty straw into a pile. Behind him Mr. Hapwood talked to Dudley. Now and again he paused, as if waiting for the animal's reply. Liam looked over. With two hands Mr. Hapwood held the horse by his halter. With short mincing steps, Dudley backed away from him. Mr. Hapwood let him do that, but he stayed close all the while, talking, his mouth close to Dudley's nostrils.

It was the way perhaps that he cast a charm, Liam thought, his voice and his breath drifting straight into an animal. Liam remembered how, on his first morning in Hell's Kitchen, Mr. Hapwood had ordered a pigeon to come down from the rafters, and it had. He remembered that when he ran by the vagrant's tent, that scarecrow of a man had screamed out words Mr. Hapwood predicted he would, about hitting Liam in the head. Suddenly Liam felt as afraid of Mr. Hapwood as he had then.

Mr. Hapwood continued to murmur to Dudley, gripping his halter tightly. Liam would never let Mr. Hapwood get that close, he promised himself, never. If he did, Mr. Hapwood might fix him with his single, fiery eye and breathe straight into him and he too might fall under Mr. Hapwood's spell.

That night, Uncle Patrick had a meeting and did not come home for supper. Liam and Alice Ann sat at the little table together, eating potato soup and thick slices of buttered bread.

Afterwards, Alice Ann sat on a chair, sewing a ribbon onto the wide-brimmed hat that Mrs. McCathery had given her yesterday. "Mrs. McCathery just bought a new hat. She says she doesn't need this one," she said to Liam as she bent over her needle.

"Jacob wants to go someplace with me tonight," Liam told her. "I'm going out."

Alice Ann looked up. "Go then, but don't be late."

Jacob was sitting on the steps of the building, waiting for Liam. "It's Forty-second Street we want and the fancy people," he said as he stood up. He ran his hand through hair that was a mass of tight, springy curls, as filled with energy as Jacob himself. He clapped his cap on. Even standing in one place on the sidewalk, Jacob jiggled back and forth, unable to be still. "C'mon," he said and started walking, taking long, impatient strides.

"The fancy people have coins in their pockets and plenty to spare," Jacob said. "They have so much money they don't know what to do with it. I read in the newspapers about a man who has a stable with carpets on the floor, from one end to the other. There's a man who invited hundreds of people to dinner and gave every woman a gold bracelet."

Where Jacob led Liam, people were milling about in front of theaters. There were men in top hats and waistcoats. A woman wore a long velvet coat. On each ear hung a bright crystal drop, dangling on a golden thread. "You see those little girls there with flowers?" Jacob asked. "I bring my little sister out selling flowers sometimes at night. I stand on the other side of the street to make sure nothing happens to her, but it looks like she's all on her own, and people tip her good. Some make their children go out in the rain or snow. When they get wet and shiver, they get the best money because people feel sorry for them. But Mama won't consider such a thing." He grinned.

"Now him," Jacob said, pointing. "We got matches. Now you watch how I handle it."

He stepped toward a man whose waistcoat was open.

Liam could see the watch chain looped across his expansive belly. In his hand was a cigar. His other hand was searching a pocket when Jacob darted up to him, holding out a lit match. The man bent down and dipped the end of his cigar into the flame. Liam saw the glint of gold cufflinks. The man sucked at the cigar. Smoke billowed. He passed a coin to Jacob.

Jacob returned to Liam's side. "That's what you do." He looked as if he had never had such a good time, and Liam thought that he seemed to like everything and everyone. Eyes eager, nodding encouragement, he gave Liam a small box with matches inside. "Try it out."

At the end of an hour, the crowds disappeared into the theater. Jacob spread the coins he had earned on his palm, and Liam did the same. "It's plenty, except I always put half away for Mama. Now, come on. That was only lesson number one. There's more I can show you, lots more," he said. "You'll see."

Before the night was over, Jacob took Liam into one building, where there were punching bags and weights, and into another with Kinetoscopes—boxes that showed moving pictures when Liam turned a crank. They sat at a counter and ate a sandwich called a hamburger, which cost five cents. In an alley behind that building, Liam saw how boys earned money by setting up pins for the men who knocked them down with bowling balls. Without paying any money at all, they stood outside of a music hall and listened to music until the music ended.

After that, they started toward home on streets that were lit here and there by gas lamps. When they passed one, light threw their own fast-moving shadows onto the ground ahead of them. They seemed to be chasing their own shadows for a few moments, and then the shadows vanished, and it was dark again.

In the apartment house, they climbed the stairs. "Let's go up to the roof. I like to go up there at night," Jacob said.

There were no stairwell lights, and there never were, Jacob told him, though a law said there should be. "I don't care," he said. "The dark doesn't bother me." He moved through the dark as swiftly and surely as a fox. Liam held onto the banister, following.

On the roof, it was brighter than on the stairs. A half-moon cast light over the pigeon coops. Standing at the roof's edge, he and Jacob could see all the way across the Hudson River. Electric advertisements rose high into the air over the New Jersey docks.

Jacob said, "It used to be all farms around here. That's what people say. It was still the outskirts of New York up until twenty years or thirty years ago. Then, when the elevated trains came up here, people started coming, too. At first it was people who didn't have much, and they lived in shanties. But now buildings are going up everywhere, and they're not shanties anymore."

Below them lights were scattered far and wide, like diamonds they might scoop up. "There are people where I lived, on Lord Clapham's land, who couldn't ever imagine this," Liam told Jacob. "There was this man named Old John, who always used to say he knew his place in the world. His place was with Lord Clapham.

He was born on Lord Clapham's estate, and he would die on it. Old John would mumble on about that to anyone willing to listen."

The morning Liam and Alice Ann had left Lord Clapham's land in the two-wheeled trap, Liam had seen Old John raking gravel on the drive, as he did every single morning. They had passed him by and turned onto the road. On each side were green hedges that formed a tunnel. The trap had flown through that tunnel, taking Liam away from all that he had ever known. In a moment of terror he had wanted to order the driver to go back.

"We fled after the Cossacks attacked our village," Jacob was saying. "The Czar would send them into Russian villages to hunt down the Jews. When they came to ours, they set houses on fire and chased people out. I remember Mama and all of us children running across a field in the snow and a Cossack charging right at us, a big saber held up, waving it with all his might. His horse stumbled and they went down, or I wouldn't be telling you the story now."

They could hear a train that whistled three times, traveling north.

"Papa was away that day." Jacob tugged at the edge of his cap. "He came back and looked for us everywhere, sure he would find us dead. We were hiding in the woods when he came searching for us. When he saw us, he ran straight at us, holding his arms out and shouting like a madman."

When Jacob asked where Liam's father was, Liam

said that his father had gone away when he was only four or five years old. "I don't know where he went," he told Jacob.

"I was five years old when we left Russia," Jacob answered. "It was a long time ago and another world. There I was in one world, and now I'm here in this one. You, too. It's the same for you."

They were in front of the pigeon coops, sticking their fingers through the wire to touch the birds. "Here, people change their lives. It's not like where we came from," Jacob said. "Here, it's like that game of football they have. You look for an opening and dive right through."

"Like on a race track," Liam answered. "You look for your opening."

On its perch, a pigeon beat its wings, fluttered up, and then came straight down. Jacob said, "If you fight hard for it, you can win the game here. At least they let you try."

They went back down the stairs. Liam followed Jacob to the second floor because they were still talking. Liam was telling him about his mother's letters and of how Colin refused to return them.

When Jacob opened the door to his apartment, Liam saw a woman—Jacob's mother, he was certain. She sat at a table, hemming a skirt. Three girls sat near her. She blinked and greeted her son, pulling hard on her needle when she did.

She had herded her children across a snowy field, chased by a huge Cossack, and now she sat at this table, looking like an ordinary, tired woman.

One of the girls was little. She called out when she saw

Jacob. She wore Jacob's own lopsided, eager grin, and Liam knew she was the little sister he took to sell flowers.

Jacob went in. The door closed.

On the floor above Jacob's apartment, Liam looked down the dark hallway toward Colin's door. A splinter of light shone under it. Colin was like a pebble in his shoe, always there, always irritating him. Colin was part of another world. In that Connemara world, the boys had held him captive. Michael Lanigan had put a knife to his throat.

And before Connemara, he had lived in Lord Clapham's world, where he was meant to keep to his station for all his life, like Old John, who asked for nothing.

But here, in this new world, people asked for everything. In this world, there were trolleys that swayed wildly on their tracks and ships that swept up and down the river. He had seen a man who swallowed fire while people threw coins at his feet.

He did not want to leave a world where anything could happen and return to the one that had trapped him. He thought of the racing pigeons that swept in ever-widening circles when released from their rooftop cages. They seemed to be testing the size of the sky. He wanted to fly higher and higher like they did.

But Uncle Patrick wouldn't want him to escape.

CHAPTER THIRTEEN

L IAM WOKE WHEN Uncle Patrick's big alarm clock sounded at six in the morning. His face to the wall, he feigned sleep while listening to his uncle dress.

Only when the front door slammed shut did he get up. In the dusky light he made his way to the front room. The floorboards were cold under his bare feet. Outside the garret windows, the sky was the color of ice. In the corner, neatly made, was the bed from Mr. Hapwood's storeroom, which Alice Ann slept on every night. Alice Ann stood in front of it and put on the hat that Mrs. McCathery had given her. Head bowed, she fixed it in place with a long hatpin. "I saw Colin last night when you were out with Jacob. He met some uppity-up in one of New York City's Irish militia companies who got him a job in the post office. Those are prize jobs, or so he said."

"So he's moving up in the world," Liam grumbled.

Alice Ann's head came up. "Are you jealous?" When

he didn't answer, Alice Ann nodded at the stove, where a pot sat. "There is porridge," she said.

"Why is there never anything but porridge? Why is there never an egg or a rasher of bacon?"

"Why are you complaining so, Liam?"

He would not say he wanted to hear nothing of some grand job Colin had found.

"Tonight there will be a ham bone in the soup if you are craving meat," Alice Ann said.

"And some old cabbage," Liam declared. "Why doesn't Uncle give you more money for food?"

"Uncle Patrick saves the money he earns at his job to buy land in Connemara. You know that. And at night he's off raising money for Ireland. That's why he's working as hard as two men now. And you don't have the right to complain about anything, Liam."

Her look accused him—of being jailed, of being fired from his position with Mr. O'Donnell, of doing all the wrong things. But before Liam could say a word in reply, Alice Ann was out the door. Liam took porridge from the pot on the stove and stood right beside it, eating. Still he shivered because the fire was almost dead and the stove was almost cold.

When his bowl was empty, Liam washed it. He took bread from the cupboard and a piece of cheese from the cold-box they kept on the fire escape. He wrapped the food in a clean rag for his mid-day meal. From the faucet in the hallway he filled the jugs kept for drinking water and the pail kept for washing up. Finally, Liam carried the two chamber pots down the five flights of stairs. At the privy in the back yard, he emptied them, holding his breath against the stink. When he rinsed them at the outside faucet, the half-frozen water turned his hands red.

Back in the building, he mounted the stairs. Rounding the third floor landing, he heard a voice. "You are slow this morning."

It was Colin, who sat on a step, staring down at him. He wore the smug grin Liam hated. In his hand were Mrs. McCathery's letters.

Liam eyed him suspiciously.

"I should not give you another chance to win these, for I said there would be no more chances if you failed."

"I don't need those letters," Liam retorted. "By now I know everything."

"By now I know everything, too," Colin said. "It's all in the letters. Your father was already married when he took your mother away. I know that."

Suddenly Liam wanted to be done with it all—with these letters and his never-ending quarrel with Colin. He wanted a new life, the one Jacob showed him.

When he shoved his way past Colin, Colin tripped him. Liam fell. One of the chamber pots smashed into the stair and cracked in half. Alice Ann would blame him for that, too. Without another thought, Liam brought the half of the chamber pot that was still in his hand down on Colin's head. Swearing, Colin released him.

Liam dashed up the stairs and into the apartment. He banged the door shut and pushed the bolt home. Through the door came Colin's shouts. "Your father, where do you think he is? I know that. Do you? The letter I have, it will tell you that."

Liam stared at the door.

Last week he had tracked the blue-eyed man, hoping he had found his father. He hadn't. But his father *was* close by. Liam was sure of it. Every day he searched for a face that was the copy of his own. His father was a groom for some rich man. Or he worked at a fine riding academy, instructing elegant ladies and gentlemen in the art of horsemanship. When Liam found him, his father would see his own face in Liam's. He'd know at once he was looking at his son. He'd shake his head in disbelief. Then he'd step toward Liam, his arms opening wide.

A strong wind shook the windows. It seemed like some big animal was trying to batter its way into the room. Colin pounded at the door, wanting in, too. "I have the letter you want," he hollered. "Open the door!"

Almost gladly, Liam shoved the bolt back. Colin waved the letters in his face, grinning. He walked into the room. "So you want the letters, after all."

Liam couldn't start his new life until he had them. "What do you want me to do?" Liam asked.

"You are late," Mr. Hapwood declared. Delmonico was already fed and watered and hitched to the wagon. Mr. Hapwood had done Liam's work for him.

From his stall, Dudley stamped his hooves and issued a high, challenging neigh. Liam looked his way. Muscles rippled along the horse's back, like a warning.

He was to ride the gray tonight, on Colin's orders. He

was to meet Colin here and take the horse into the yard and mount.

Colin had heard that the horse was crazed and seen him in the yard with Mr. Hapwood. Only twenty minutes ago, he had issued his challenge— "Are you not the grand horseman, the son of Lord Clapham's head groom? Prove it to me. Ride him."

Liam eyed the saddle that lay across a sawhorse. Yes, there was a saddle. That is what he had told Colin. It was a McClellan army saddle, given to Mr. Hapwood by a cousin who had served in the cavalry. Mr. Hapwood took pride in it. Even though it was never used, he polished its leather until it shone.

Tonight he would put that saddle on Dudley and ride him. In return, Colin would give him every letter. That would end things for good. He would never speak to Colin again.

Now, at Mr. Hapwood's command, Liam took hold of Delmonico's bridle and led him outside. Two chickens, their feathers ruffled, faced into a wind. Overhead, in this same wind, clouds skidded toward the east, where the morning sky was light.

When Mr. Hapwood said, "All right, climb on up," Liam hoisted himself onto the bench they shared. The wagon left the yard.

Two blocks away, along a gutter where dirty water ran, a man urged three sheep toward the wide-open doors of a slaughterhouse. The sheep did not know they were going to their death. They weren't afraid of that. They were only afraid of the stick the man waved.

Mr. Hapwood's wagon pulled onto West End Avenue and headed north. Liam tucked his hands into his armpits to warm them. Had it ever been so cold on an April day in Ireland?

Finally, on Sixty-fourth Street, Mr. Hapwood drew the wagon to a stop near a large warehouse that was unlike any of the others. On its roof was a small replica of the Statue of Liberty. Mr. Hapwood pointed to the statue. "You seen Liberty out to sea. Up here, she shrunk some. Dang if she didn't. Liberty Warehouse is what she's called, this here building, and putting on grand airs is what she does, with that Statue of Liberty up on top of her."

Mr. Hapwood drew a paper from a satchel he always kept by him. "We gonna load up here for a Mr. Emerson," he said. Liam knew that the paper in his hands was an inventory that listed the items they would transport. "You stay put 'til I get this straightened out."

Minutes went by. There were sounds—the clatter of traffic, a flutter of pigeons, the high barking of a dog, and then, gradually increasing in volume, a clanging of bells. When Liam turned around in his seat, he saw a fire wagon. It rounded a corner. Three horses galloped side by side, pulling it, their legs lifting up and coming down.

With a great clatter the fire wagon drew close. Delmonico began to fidget. When it passed, Delmonico stomped the ground and their wagon lurched. Then, suddenly, Delmonico was on the move himself, his ears tilted in the direction of the running horses. Quickly, Liam slid into Mr. Hapwood's place. The wagon rocked as Delmonico broke into a trot. Liam braced his shoulders to keep his seat. He grabbed for the reins, but before he could tighten them, the horse picked up its pace. In moments, the trot became an all-out gallop.

Dimly, Liam was aware of things that rushed by in a whirl—a woman with a bundle of clothes on her head, the overflowing ash cans along the curbs, a boy on roller skates, three gaping men—

Things Mr. Hapwood had once said rushed through Liam's mind, too. Delmonico had been a fire horse—a fire horse would run at the clanging of fire bells, the scent of racing horses, the sight of men in helmets. He was a fire horse.

Liam sawed on the reins. Shaking his head, Delmonico fought the bit. A few blocks ahead of them, flames spiraled into the air. Delmonico pulled all the harder. The wood of the wagon gave a groan as they turned another corner. Liam stared at the bright sheen of sweat along the horse's back. In that very moment the wagon's inside wheel went careening up a curb. The wagon tilted to the side. Liam heard the splintering of wood, and he went flying into the air, the ground coming up at him. There was a tin can and a stick and scattered rocks. And then his shoulder scraped along gravel. In some part of his brain he was aware of searing pain and aware that Delmonico was going down, too.

When Liam looked up, the horse was caught in a tangle of reins. He was thrashing his legs, trying to rise. This was the way horses broke their legs, tripping as they struggled, crazy with fright.

Somehow, dizzily, Liam scrambled toward Delmonico. In a moment, he was straddling the horse's head. He leaned over and looked into Delmonico's terrified eyes.

"Steady now," he said. "Easy, easy, Delmonico. I will tell you that it does no good to get up, not yet. We'll get you undone in time, don't you know. Steady now."

The horse's lips were drawn back, as if he were trying to speak.

"Hey!" Another boy had joined him, a skinny-faced boy with a protruding Adam's apple. He sat down alongside Liam on Delmonico's neck and said, "You're a right bloody mess, you are!"

Liam put a hand to his head. There was blood. He ran his tongue over his lips and tasted it.

Mr. Hapwood crouched on the ground by Liam. With a folded handkerchief he staunched the blood that flowed above Liam's right eye. "For a minute there, when I didn't see anybody right side up, it gave me quite a start," he said. "I thought maybe Delmonico was a goner, and you, too. I thought maybe I'd seen the last of you."

Mr. Hapwood was still breathing hard from running. His face was damp with perspiration. "Don't you worry now," he said "I'll get you out of this mess." He bent over Liam and ran his fingers along Liam's skull. "Your head's in one piece."

Hastily, flinching, Liam drew back, away from him.

"Don't mean to hurt you none. You got dirt in those scrapes though. Best to get that out straight away. Don't want anything in there, festering. We'll deal with that in another minute. Right now, I gotta deal with Delmonico."

While Liam made his way to the curb and sat down, three hefty men, from a circle of onlookers, stepped forward and helped Mr. Hapwood get Delmonico to his feet. Lightheaded, Liam watched, gripping the curb tightly. Only yesterday he had feared that if Mr. Hapwood came as close he just had, he would cast a spell on him. Was this a spell, this floating feeling?

In a few minutes, Delmonico was back up on his feet, shaking his head as if he were dizzy, too. Meanwhile, people were retrieving Mr. Hapwood's scattered possessions. "Thank you for helping out here," Mr. Hapwood said to one person and to another. A girl picked up the water jug that Mr. Hapwood always kept in the wagon. She gave it to him. "Thank you, kindly," he said. The jug in one hand, he knelt down next to Liam.

"Close your eyes. Lift your chin up," he commanded as he poured a thin stream of water across Liam's face. He could be dousing a flame.

When Liam opened his eyes, he was staring at Mr. Hapwood's scar. Mr. Hapwood dabbed at Liam's cuts with a handkerchief and said, "I been hard on you sometimes. There are times I want to be hard on you, on any boy who looks like you, that's all."

"Why?"

"Why? There was a mob of boys after me one time. That's why."

"Why were they after you?" Liam asked, before closing his eyes again. The world was spinning.

"You all right? Maybe I got to get a doctor?"

Liam shook his head, no. Eyes closed, he heard Mr. Hapwood talk in a calm and steady voice, the one somebody might use when telling a fairy tale to a child.

"The way it started is, a man goes into a store to buy a cigar, a black man. He comes out again, and there is a white fella that is bothering his wife. They start scrappin', like men might do—a situation like that. The black man cuts the white man with this penknife he got. Then, what do you know, the man ups and dies, and it turns out he's a policeman. Had no uniform on, so the black fella was unaware of that."

Liam raised his head. There were amber flecks in Mr. Hapwood's eyes that he had never noticed before.

"The evening after the funeral, why mobs are pulling black people off streetcars, chasing them down on the sidewalks. They are goin' after any black man in sight. Six or seven of them get hold of me, one just your size, a few of them older, one about my own age and built like a bull. Gonna string me up on a lamp post, set me on fire, that's what they are saying, and they've got a torch."

Mr. Hapwood stopped talking until Liam said, "What happened?"

"I'm handy with my fists and for awhile I hold my own. Then they get the better of me. They get me down and are swiping the torch at my face and hammering at me. I'm thinking I am done for, but next thing I know, Mrs. McCathery is right alongside me—some old board in her hand that she ripped off a fence. She swings it at those boys. She gives one a good whack on the head.

Course you can't get her to admit that, not nowadays you can't. It doesn't bear talking about, is how she puts it. She doesn't believe in people whacking people, she tells me, and she only made that one exception that one time for my sake." Mr. Hapwood gave a horse-like snort, laughing. "Startled 'em some," he said, "seeing a lady come after them, and Irish like they was. Gave me a chance to get back up on my feet and start fighting them off me again."

"You got away?"

"Well, that's plain to see." Mr. Hapwood folded up his handkerchief. It was damp and bloody. "So are the marks they left on my face. I gotta look twice at myself in the mirror before I know who I am."

So that explained the scars, the half-closed eye, and Mr. Hapwood's torn ear. "Well, if one of those boys looked just like you that time, we'll say that's his fault, not yours," Mr. Hapwood declared. "You had nothing to do with any of it. It's time I said that loud and clear."

He lifted Liam's shirt and poked at his ribs. "None of them is broke as far as I see," he announced. He let the shirt fall and said, "Since that time me and Mrs. McCathery, why we been partners. We bought Dudley together, and the two of us are putting money down on the lot that runs between our places. In cahoots on all this business end of things. She's one get-ahead woman, and me, why I don't like to stand still neither, so we make a pair."

Next, Liam was getting to his feet, with Mr. Hapwood supporting his elbow and saying, "Took four of us to get

Delmonico up. You are doing a sight better than him anyhow."

Mr. Hapwood checked one wagon wheel and then another. The wagon itself was battered, its sides punched in. There was a rip in the boards that bore the words *Hapwood & Co., Transport.*

"Get you home first and after that I'll come on back up here, get the job done myself."

"I can go on with you."

"You sure? You look worn out to me."

But Mr. Hapwood was already turning the wagon toward the north and the warehouse. The clanging of wheels on stone rattled Liam's brain, and he hardly heard what Mr. Hapwood was saying, ". . . St. Benedict the Moor Church, over on West Fifty-third there, that's where I attend. Some years back, that church was the first black mission church north of the Mason Dixon Line."

Liam stared at him—a Catholic church. He was talking of going to a Catholic church. Mr. Hapwood would kneel before a priest. On Sunday he might take the host; on Friday, confess; in Lent, pray the Stations of the Cross and fast.

"On Bleecker Street is where it was in my Granddaddy's time, St. Benedict's. On Bleecker when my Granddaddy come up from Alabama on the Underground Railway— you heard of that particular railroad? Mister Cornelius Vanderbilt didn't build that railroad line." He gave his barking laugh. "No, sir. That line, blacks was in charge, and Quakers and such was helping out—white folks who didn't want slavery neither."

He glanced over at Liam, a worried look on his face. "You doin' okay there?"

"I'm all right," Liam answered. Mr. Hapwood was talking as never before, Liam realized, to keep him from thinking about the wagon's crashing and about all of his cuts and scrapes.

"Then later on, with black people coming up here to Hell's Kitchen? Why St. Benedict's went and followed them. Churches, schools, what have you," he went on, "why they just follow us wherever we go, tail right behind—Hell's Kitchen or wherever. Might be Harlem before long. Some black people are moving up there."

There was a shake of the reins that brought no response from Delmonico, whose head hung down in exhaustion and shame. "Some fine buildings in Harlem," Mr. Hapwood added. "Might look into it myself one fine day."

Liam had never heard so much from Mr. Hapwood, and what had he known about him then? Nothing. Nothing except Mr. Hapwood's fierce look and his scars and his pride, and that he seemed to know everything there was to know about horses.

The wagon rattled on. The voice rattled on. "You ever notice all the churches around where we live? Not only St. Benedicts for the black people. They got a German church, a Greek church, an Italian church, a Russian church, Baptist Church, every kind of church. Well, we got every kind of people, so there is going to be every kind of church, I expect."

"You said it was the devil's territory, Hell's Kitchen. You never mentioned churches that day," Liam replied.

Mr. Hapwood gave him a grin. He shook his head. "Well, I do remember saying that. I do remember wanting to have a go at you. But the truth of the matter is, if you got a tavern on one corner in Hell's Kitchen, why you got yourself a church in the next block. If you got a bad man, there is gonna be a good one standin' by, generally speaking. That's how it works most every place, I expect. Hell's Kitchen, too."

They were pulling in by Liberty Warehouse. Stopping, Mr. Hapwood turned to Liam. "You stay put. Rest. I'll be back soon. I won't be long."

Descending, Mr. Hapwood stood in front of Delmonico and took hold of his bridle. He said into the horse's face, "Don't you go nowhere this time, hear? You aren't a fire horse no more."

It wasn't a witch-like pronouncement. It was anyone's strict warning. And Mr. Hapwood wasn't a fiend, but someone who might say a Hail Mary or sit in a pew on a Sunday morning. And what had Mr. Hapwood thought about him? That he could go mad on some dark night like the boys who chased him once, that he could swipe a torch across a black man's face—shrieking and gleeful as a devil?

Chapter Fourteen

THE STABLE WAS DARK. Colin raised the lantern he held as Liam entered Dudley's stall. When Dudley skittered to the side, Liam remembered that the horse had once cornered a stable hand in a stall and then attacked. Liam scooted forward until he faced Dudley head on. Dudley pinned his ears back and curled a lip, but, in the end, he took the slices of apple Liam offered. Next Liam slipped a lead rope on the training halter that Dudley wore.

As he did all this, Liam talked steadily to Dudley in the even voice Mr. Hapwood used. The horse flicked his ears forward, listening to what Liam related—that he had stayed in bed until everyone else was asleep and then crept out of his room and out of the building. Nobody had seen him because nobody was awake, Liam told him. He did not mention that he had been so tired and so sore from the day's accident that he had to force himself onto his feet.

"We're going to have ourselves a ride," Liam said

finally. "It's time to go." He tapped on Dudley's nose. "Now step back," Liam ordered. "Back," he repeated in the firm, gruff voice Mr. Hapwood used.

Muscles shuddering along his flanks, ears twitching uneasily, the gray backed up. In the corner of Dudley's stall, the yellow dog scrambled to her feet and gave a yip. In the stall next to them, Delmonico turned, watching what was going on with keen interest. When Liam cross-tied Dudley to a post in the center of the stable, Dudley pulled back on the rope, cocking a leg, ready to kick.

"Get the saddle on him," Colin said.

"Well, get it for me then. Over there." Liam pointed. "And the reins on that peg above it."

Colin handed Liam the saddle, and Liam said, "Mr. Hapwood has not put a saddle on him yet." He hoisted it across Dudley's withers before sliding it into place, smoothing the hairs down. Dudley's tail lashed back and forth. His ears went perfectly flat. "See how I do it, so the saddle won't rub you wrong," he murmured to the horse. "I won't hurt you. I won't ever do anything to hurt you. Don't worry."

Liam felt the tension in Dudley's muscles when he ran his hand across the horse's shoulder. He looked at Colin. "He's like a firecracker, with the fuse burning down right under my hand."

On their way home that afternoon, Mr. Hapwood had told Liam that the man who first bought Dudley used a bridle with chinstraps that would choke off a horse's wind. There had been regular whippings and a twisted wire snaffle that had cut Dudley's mouth.

"All that, and then they'd go and take his food and his water away for days at a time," Mr. Hapwood had snapped. "Some folks want to drive the will right out of an animal, make him submit. What they get is either a horse with no life in him at all or a half-crazed beast that won't do nothin' it's told. Me, I'm just starting all over with Dudley—no spurs, no whips, no bit even, not for some time yet. I'm gonna get his trust back. Why, if I don't have him racing at three, he'll be racing at four. If that's good enough for him, it's good enough for me. Slow's the answer."

Slow.

Liam could hear Mr. Hapwood's voice clearly. It was as if he were standing right next to Dudley. And Liam seemed to be talking to Mr. Hapwood, not to Colin, when he said, "I won't attempt a bridle and bit. Hooves will fly if I try to put a bit in his mouth. Give me the reins."

He took the reins from Colin and clipped them onto the halter rings. The gray tossed his head and shied away. "Mr. Hapwood would have none of this," Liam told Colin.

He could quit now and put the animal back in its stall beside Delmonico. The old yellow dog would curl up again and go to sleep. The dog would not be standing on her bowed legs, staring warily like she did now.

He said to Colin, hesitating, "Dudley isn't ready."

"You are the one who is not ready. You are a coward."

Liam glared at him. He pulled on the girth, tightening the saddle, and then jumped back, out of reach of

Dudley's nervous, shifting hooves. "I told you I'll ride Dudley, and I will. You'd never have the nerve for it."

He walked Dudley to the open stable door, where he cinched the girth tighter. He had once seen a saddle slip and a man go upside down, and he didn't want to be looking at Dudley's belly on this ride. Dudley edged away from Liam and reared his head high, tugging at the reins. He stomped his hooves. "Easy," Liam said, "easy."

When Liam led the jittery animal outside, Colin followed. The lantern was in his left hand. In his right was a crate. The moon had come up. It was almost full and far up in the cold sky now. When a cloud crossed over it and the night grew darker, Colin held the lantern higher. In its light Liam could see Dudley's breath stream from his nostrils, like smoke. For an instant he imagined that smoke came from deep in Dudley's belly, where there was a smoldering, fuming fire.

They crossed through the yard and entered the training ring. Colin set the crate down. "Get on up."

Without even a bit to control the gray, there was no way he could stay on his back, Liam knew, and he dreaded the fall that was to come. His head and body throbbed from this afternoon's fall. He hunched his shoulders and said, "I'll walk him first."

"Walk him?"

"To work his muscles before riding him. It's the way it's done."

"You are scared of him. That is the truth of it."

"What do you know about horses?"

But what Colin said was true, Liam admitted to himself. Dudley had trampled a groom—hooves striking and cracking bone.

The horse skittered nervously behind Liam as Liam set out. They circled once. Passing Colin, Liam sensed his impatience. Colin might begin at any moment to shout at him, like the man who had shouted at the sheep that morning. When that man's high yelps herded the sheep toward their own death, the animals had answered with hopeless bleating and run mindlessly along the gutter.

Mindless sheep. This was mindless, this circling. He would circle once more—and only once. Then he would ride Dudley, and then it would be done.

Overhead, between the clouds, Liam could see stars. On the ship, he and Mr. Gavin had seen those same stars. That night they had talked of Cuchullain and Ireland's fearless warriors, but Mr. Gavin had said he would be a warrior only if his hand were forced.

Liam wondered if he could have taken a pike himself and swung it at one of Cromwell's men. The boys who had swung a torch at Mr. Hapwood hadn't been afraid of burning flesh. Or had they been afraid? Afterward, sitting at supper with a mother or a little brother, were they silent, terrified by what they had done? At night did they dream of it and startle awake with a scream lodged in their throats?

Who were they?

Liam's feet went steadily forward but his thoughts scattered every which way. He could not seem to stop his mind's jumbled racing.

Mr. Gavin had wanted to be an astronomer and to spend his life watching stars. But no plain Irish boy from Clare or Kerry or Cork or Sligo or Connemara or anywhere else in Ireland could do such a thing.

The Irish and the English were enemies. England took all it could from the Irish, but once Mum had seen two Irish men drive a landlord's cattle off a cliff in Kildare. Later, on the beach, she had discovered their broken bodies and cried. She cried, she said, for all the beasts and the innocent people who had died in the centuries-old battles, killed by the English and by the Irish alike.

He was Irish and English, both. He hadn't denied his father when the boys tried to make him do it. He hadn't denied his mother when Uncle Patrick attacked her with his hard words.

Fiona was Irish, but she had never cared that Liam's father was English, the way Colin did. It had never mattered to her at all. He remembered how, once, on the day they climbed Clydesdale Hill, he had pointed to cattle grazing far below them and said a witch had turned them into mice. Fiona had laughed, and when she did, wind snatched her brown, curly hair, making it fly every which way. She stretched out both hands. He had taken them and pulled her toward him.

It was always that simple with Fiona, not like this.

Liam took a thin breath. He willed his mind to be still. Colin was just ahead of him now, the crate at his feet.

When Liam halted the horse, Colin backed away. For a mere moment, in the light of the lantern, he and Liam stared at each other. And then Liam's right foot was in the stirrup. A violent tremor went through Dudley. The horse humped his back. Liam hoisted himself up in one swift motion. Stiff-legged, Dudley leapt forward.

"Steady!"

Before the word was even out, the gray was in the air.

He reared. Then he seemed to bend entirely in half. He bucked to the right and left. Dudley went one way and Liam went another. It was as if a giant hand had simply descended from the sky, ripped Liam off the animal, and tossed him carelessly down. Liam slid along the ground. He smelled dirt and grass. He felt his britches tearing. Ahead of him, the gray horse ran, bucking still, tail whipping. Colin ran, too. In Colin's hand the lantern swung from side to side. Light ricocheted.

As Liam clambered to his feet, he saw how, a half a dozen yards away, Colin pressed himself against the side of the corral. The horse was directly in front of him, crowding him. As if he were trying to surrender to some enemy soldier on a battlefield, Colin raised his hands straight up. Dudley's head snaked forward. Colin screamed, the lantern fell to the ground, and glass shattered.

In the moon's uneven light, Liam saw how Colin lay sprawled under the horse's belly, feet lashing out, as if he hoped to kick the horse away. The gray squealed.

Liam did not know how he managed to grasp the reins and drag Dudley off Colin. When Dudley reared up, his hooves sliced at the air. Like a boxer in a ring, Liam spun away. Again and again, the horse whipped his head. Liam dug his heels in, shouting at Colin. "Are you all right? Colin! Say something!"

Colin rolled onto his side. An arm stirred. Liam moved toward the gate of the yard, yanking on Dudley's reins. Yanking back, quivering with rage, Dudley unwillingly followed. They entered the stable. In spite of the panic he felt, as he closed the horse in his stall, Liam tried to talk to him in an even voice to calm him. But in the dark, his voice trembled with fear, and Dudley snorted and stomped in reply.

Liam ran to the field. He knelt by Colin. "Are you all right?"

"I am not."

"Where are you hurt?" Colin only groaned. "Where does it hurt?" Liam asked a second time.

Colin's breath came in a low panting. "You cannot believe the pain, all over, but the leg. It's the leg, I think."

When Liam ran his hand lightly down the leg, he found the large tear in the trousers above the knee. He jumped when he touched a raw bone that protruded through the skin. Blood flowed onto his fingers. Sickened, he pulled his hand away. But then he drew a breath and forced his hand down again. He shredded a strip of cloth from Colin's torn trousers and tied a tourniquet above the wound. That done, Liam took off his jacket and covered Colin with it to keep him warm. "I'll get help," he said.

"Don't leave."

"I'll go straight to your father. I'll be back in minutes."

"You better come back!" When Liam stood, Colin's voice rose to a shrill pitch. "The letters are yours, but only if you return. Not until then. Hear me? Not until then!"

"You think I would leave you here?"

Colin turned his head aside, moaning again, and Liam said, "This has nothing to do with the letters." Clouds touched the moon. In the light that sifted through them, Colin's face was shriveled. "Colin?"

There was no answer.

"Colin!"

Liam was on his feet. He was running.

Snow had begun to fall. Wind shuffled the flakes. Without his coat, Liam shivered. This April was vicious cold. It made no sense—tonight nothing did, not the biting wind and snow, not the ride he had taken on the gray, not the blood.

CHAPTER FIFTEEN

MR. GAVIN, MRS. MCCATHERY, Alice Ann, Uncle
Patrick, Mr. Hapwood, and a doctor all crowded around
Colin in the apartment. Liam pressed against the wall.
He wished he were invisible. He did not want any one of
them to turn to him with questions about what had hap-
pened. So far, only Mr. Hapwood had asked anything.
That had been an hour ago, after Mrs. McCathery and
Mr. Gavin had shouted for Mr. Hapwood's help and he
had rushed out of his house by the stable.

"What you two been up to?" he had asked Liam when
he came into the corral. Glancing in Colin's direction,
and at Mr. Gavin and Mrs. McCathery, who crouched
by him, he had pulled Liam aside. "Dudley—I just seen
him in his stall. He's got a saddle on him."

When Liam said nothing, Mr. Hapwood had said,
"You better got some kind of answer. What you and that
other boy been doing with Dudley?"

"Riding him."

"He's not ready for that."

"He made me do it," Liam told him. "Colin did."

"Made you?" Mr. Hapwood said nothing for a few moments, but then he brought his face close to Liam's. "You doin' just exactly what he tells you, like that boy owns you? Owns you? That it? Ha! Talk to my granddaddy—scars on his back from one side to the other, and two children sold away from under him. Go and hear him out about a man owning another man. Nobody owns you. You're not gonna be giving me any such talk as that."

Liam shrank away from his fury.

"You got no right to such talk," Mr. Hapwood had sputtered, "no right, not unless you been bought and sold."

In the end, they had carried Colin across the field in a blanket that sagged under Colin's weight. Liam and Mr. Gavin had held onto it in the back. Holding it in front, Uncle Patrick and Mr. Hapwood synchronized their strides so they would not jolt Colin any more than necessary. "Easy now," Mr. Hapwood had said as he took a long step over a shallow ditch. Nodding, Uncle Patrick took a step just like his. The two of them worked in tandem, like a matched pair of horses.

Liam put his right foot forward when they did, too. By the light of the lantern that Mrs. McCathery held up, he saw the snow, flakes flying in all directions. Walking Dudley, his thoughts had flown in all directions like that, Liam admitted to himself. He had been so afraid then that he hadn't been able to think straight.

But it was Colin who had been hurt, not him. It was

Colin who cried out in pain when they carried him up the stairs. It was Colin who lay on the bed now. He was vomiting into the pan that Mrs. McCathery held for him. When she moved away, the doctor took her place. At the wrist, the doctor's cuffs were frayed, but his long hands were clean. They moved expertly along Colin's leg.

When the doctor was done with his examination, Mrs. McCathery and Mr. Gavin slipped a nightshirt over Colin's head. "Is there a neighbor with a telephone?" the doctor asked. "Someone who can call?" At the shaking of heads, he said, "Well, is there someone we can send for an ambulance then? We have to get him to a hospital."

"Send me." It was Mr. Hapwood who stepped forward. Uncle Patrick studied him as the doctor said, "Roosevelt Hospital, it's only a dozen blocks away."

"I know the place," Mr. Hapwood replied.

"They have an operating theater there. It's our best bet. Now run."

Liam stepped toward the bed and picked up Colin's clothes, which Mrs. McCathery had set down on the floor. At a table by the wall, he shielded his hands from view. No one saw him take his mother's four letters from Colin's trouser pocket. Quickly Liam slipped them inside his waistband. He tucked his shirt in again.

Liam walked out of the room and into the hallway, where Mr. Gavin faced the doctor. "How can you say that?" he was asking. His question was an angry accusation.

The doctor wet his lips but said nothing. Mr. Gavin glared at him. "He must not lose the leg. Don't say he will. Young he is, young still! God have mercy, the leg nothing but a stump!"

Liam flinched—*a leg cut off?*

Shaking his head, the doctor went back into the apartment. Mr. Gavin did not move. "One son died at sea," he said in a hollow voice. "And now another there is with a leg gone." He looked at Liam.

"You remind me of Fergus. Your age he was when he died three years ago—at sea, fishing. And about your size, small, don't you know, not like the others. And something there was of Fergus in the very look on your face, the day I first saw you . . ."

After a silence, Mr. Gavin said, "To this day I see him falling from the boat and myself plunging in after him. Didn't I swim with all my might, but there was nothing for it. The storm blew the church doors open in the town that morning and blew the candles out. People knew someone had died in that very instant."

It was because he looked like Fergus that Mr. Gavin had given him Fergus's boots and taught him things, Liam realized. Mr. Gavin's eyes were searching his face now. "What part did you play in this business with the horse, lad?"

"Colin dared me to ride Dudley," Liam answered, "and I did it, but Dudley attacked Colin after throwing me off."

"Dared you, did he, and so you wanted to prove yourself. Is that it? And it was you and Colin, all these weeks—having a go at each other on the ship, and here too, no doubt. And part of your glorious battling, was it, this business with that monster?"

Liam dropped his eyes. Mr. Gavin's voice was as sharp as a knife. "That mad horse all but killed another lad, did you not know that?"

"I knew about it," Liam admitted.

"That the horse was a danger, it was a thing you knew. Ah, sure you did. Sure you knew all that, and it did not matter to you."

Mr. Gavin slipped back into the apartment while, below, the front door opened. There were voices, Mr. Hapwood's voice and others. It would be the men with the ambulance. Liam had no wish to see Colin on a stretcher. He sprinted up the steps, away from it all.

Colin had chased him up the same steps that morning. It was as if Colin were chasing him still, seeking revenge. Liam had sworn that he would never have anything to do with Colin after riding Dudley. But it was not over yet. Colin would forfeit a leg. That was the price Colin paid. Liam thought that in the end he would pay a price, too. Mr. Gavin blamed him. Mr. Hapwood did. He blamed himself.

He pushed open the door to the apartment. Inside, in the dark, Liam searched for the matches he knew were on the table. His hands scrabbled along the rough wood until they touched the box. He pried the mantle from the kerosene lamp. He struck a match, lit the wick, and replaced it. Bending close to the faint light, he read the letters.

Carefully Liam lay the letters on the embers inside the

stove. In seconds, a fire flared. He balled up the envelopes and threw them in and watched them burn as well.

All that he had done—and the fire burned itself out in seconds. All that he had done—and it was worthless.

South Africa.

His father was in South Africa. With an angry shove, Liam closed the stove's small door, walked to the windows and placed both palms on the frigid glass. He could make out a swirl of snow. He looked up but could see no stars, only blackness. This afternoon, while Delmonico plodded toward home, Mr. Hapwood had said that runaway slaves might travel in the dead of winter, their feet wrapped in rags, with only the stars to guide them. Liam wondered what they had done when the stars vanished, on a night like this.

On this starless night, everything had gone wrong—the gray horse had attacked Colin and now his father had vanished.

He was still at the window when Alice Ann walked in with Uncle Patrick. "That horse is a danger," Uncle Patrick said when Liam turned. "In league with the devil, he is."

Liam thought to say it was not Dudley's fault and that he should never have taken the horse out of its stall to begin with. If he said that, there would be a strapping, he guessed, and so he said nothing.

"Go to bed," Uncle Patrick told Alice Ann when she yawned. His voice was almost kind. "There is nothing more to do for that boy, not tonight certainly." Then he was gone, into the room he and Liam shared.

Alice Ann came to the window and looked out as Liam was doing. She wrapped her arms around herself and said, "Uncle Patrick told Mr. Hapwood he must kill the horse. Mr. Hapwood only gave Uncle that look of his, as if Uncle were some child acting up."

"Uncle can't order Mr. Hapwood around. He won't let anybody order him around."

"Mrs. McCathery said that Uncle was right, that the horse might kill some other boy who came too near him," Alice Ann said. "She couldn't bear the thought."

Liam shook his head, resisting the idea.

"It's her horse, too," Alice Ann persisted. "They bought him together, Mr. Hapwood and Mrs. McCathery did."

"I know that," Liam snapped. In the same angry voice, he said, "I know where Father went."

Alice Ann gave a start. The tired look left her face.

"South Africa. Father fought there in the Boer Wars, fought for England. He was hurt. He lost an eye and three fingers on a hand, and they released him from service, but he stayed there all they same. He's raising horses. And he has had another child."

"There is a new baby?" Alice Ann murmured.

"A boy. He's a few months old."

A man from Kildare who fought beside his father in South Africa had told his mother this after he returned to Ireland. In her last letter, Mum had revealed it to Mrs. McCathery—*It quite took my breath away, the thought of another baby that was William's but not my own. Didn't pain shoot through my heart all over again?*

Alice Ann asked, "How do you know all this?"

"I saw a letter from Mum, a letter she wrote to Mrs. McCathery."

"You saw a letter?" Alice Ann seemed to be asking how he had seen Mum's letter, but Liam didn't answer. He didn't want to tell her.

Alice Ann said softly, "He's far away then. Sometimes I'd think, like you, that we'd find Father here."

"He's not here," Liam replied, his voice almost a whisper, like hers. "He'll never come here. We'll never see him again."

Alice Ann bit at her lip. She was blinking back tears. When she stepped back, there was only Liam's single reflection in the window. Past it, the snow continued to fall. In the stable yard, it was covering Colin's footprints and his own, and the imprint of Dudley's hooves. Their father was gone, but Liam wanted to think that, by morning, when snow had erased those wild marks, the problems surrounding Dudley would be erased, too. They would vanish. It would be over.

He didn't really believe that. He stared at his reflection. What else would happen?

Mr. Hapwood said, "You are the one got Dudley into this fix. It was your doin', so it's your job now. Go on, take the gun."

Reluctantly, Liam did.

Next to an apple tree in Mr. Hapwood's yard, he and Liam had already dug a grave. While morning turned to afternoon, they had worked without stopping. The day was an April day, and nothing like the day before, when snow had fallen. It was bright and warm. Liam and Mr. Hapwood had even removed their jackets and rolled their shirtsleeves up. Their jackets were slung over a low branch of the apple tree. Dudley was tied there on a long rope now, and he nosed at a coat sleeve, curious.

Mr. Hapwood took oats from a feedbag on the ground. He clucked at Dudley and held the oats out, his palm flat as a plate. Dudley stepped toward him. Twitching his nose, distrustful, the gray snuffled at the treat.

Mr. Hapwood's voice was gruff. "Hold that gun between his eyes, Liam, right next to his forehead. Leave an inch of room between him and the end of that pistol maybe, but no more than that. Go on."

Liam did as he was told. He held the large, heavy gun with two hands and pointed it at Dudley.

"That gun's powerful. It'll do the job. All you got to do is pull on the trigger."

As Mr. Hapwood said that, the gray horse raised his head, shoving the gun out of his way. The gesture was almost careless, as if Dudley believed he could simply tell Liam to leave him be and go away and Liam would.

For the second time, Mr. Hapwood offered the horse oats, and again Dudley mouthed his palm. "He don't know nothin' about what you're gonna do," Mr. Hapwood told Liam. "Go ahead and do it. What are you waitin' for now?"

The barrel of the gun lay almost directly on Dudley's forehead. Liam closed his eyes. His heart beat hard. It felt as if someone were pounding on the wall of his chest from inside, trapped there and desperate, wanting out.

The barrel of the gun dropped down. "I cannot," he said. "I can't do it."

Mr. Hapwood snatched the gun from Liam's hand. He frowned. "Neither can I. I can't—no more than you. That's a fact. Don't got it in my heart. He was coming along nice. You seen him at the end of that rope when I put him through his paces. You seen his form, and how he'd—"

The sound of the shot came and then, instantaneously, the sound of two more shots. Dudley's head reared. Liam saw the whites of his eyes and heard the beginning of a sound that had no finish, a cut-off scream. In the same moment, Dudley's legs buckled. Mr. Hapwood was finishing his sentence: "—how he'd move so true like a fine bred animal." He jerked a rag out of his trouser pocket and began wiping the gun down.

Liam's mouth had gone dry. He had not fired the shot and yet he had. He remembered saddling Dudley last night and telling the horse that he would not hurt him. "I am sorry," he said.

"Sorry?" Mr. Hapwood growled. "Well, now."

Dudley sprawled beside his grave, blood seeping from his head. Three times Liam swallowed, afraid he might be sick. He remembered seeing Michael Lanigan's pony outside the church the day after he had clipped its forelock, mane, and tail. Dispirited and cold, it had stood in the rain. There had been that pony at the very start. Now there was the gray horse. The animals had nothing to do with what lay between Michael Lanigan or Colin and himself.

"The man who had Dudley first, well dang if he didn't beat on him when he was wanting to teach Dudley to stand still." Mr. Hapwood's rough whispery voice was like sandpaper. "If that isn't sheer foolishness."

Mr. Hapwood crouched down, put a hand on Dudley's neck, and looked into the horse's eyes. Dudley did not look back. His gaze was fixed on the blue sky. Mr. Hapwood said, "He never got to where I wanted him — knowing he wasn't nobody's slave anymore."

Mr. Hapwood stood. He snatched their two jackets from the tree branch and threw Liam his. Giving Liam a single, bitter glance, he put on the other one. "Maybe you better go on and get out of my sight. 'Bout now I don't have no need of you or anybody else. Most especially you, you want the truth of the matter. Go on."

It would do no good to say *I'm sorry* again. "I'm going," he said instead.

He crossed over the road and into the stable yard. Except for occasional patches of snow that dotted the grass, there was little trace of yesterday's bizarre snowstorm. It was as if yesterday had never happened.

But the crate Liam had used when he mounted Dudley was right where he and Colin had left it. Liam stood beside it and examined the trampled marks Dudley had made. The horse had been alive then, twisting and mad. In the mud were Colin's running footprints and his own, too. All of last night's story was written here, plain to see.

CHAPTER SIXTEEN

AT THE BATHHOUSE, Liam and Jacob waited in a long line. When they finally reached the head of the line, a man gave each of them a towel and a bar of soap. "You got dressing rooms down that hallway and showers in there," he said, "and you got fifteen minutes, no more than that."

Before they went into their separate stalls, Jacob waved his bar of soap under Liam's nose — "Colgate soap and hot water, that's what will make an American out of you! You'll come out of that shower and you'll be somebody new."

Water came down like rain that was miraculously hot. Liam turned his face up. He lathered his body with soap. The water poured over him. It felt as if he were washing away the scrapes and bruises on his legs and torso and arms, and thoughts of Dudley and Colin, too. It felt as if he were, in fact, turning into somebody new.

But during the walk home, he and Jacob talked about nothing but Dudley and Colin and of what had happened three nights before. Jacob said, "I wouldn't want to be in your shoes. But you're wearing those shoes, and you just have to keep on walking. You can only leave it behind if you keep walking ahead."

And then Liam was in the apartment and Uncle Patrick was there, sitting on one of the three chairs, reading a newspaper, *The Irish World*. "Where have you been?" he asked without looking up. He continued to trace the words he read with the tip of his finger.

"To the baths with my friend Jacob," Liam answered.

"A jug of water and a basin is not enough for you, or the tin tub Mrs. McCathery would lend us if you would haul it up here?"

"A nickel is all it cost me," Liam said.

"A nickel is it? And off you go to baths like a fancy man." His uncle lowered the paper. A strange light came into the eyes. "And tonight were you spending the money that Mr. Hapwood paid you?"

"Jacob gave it to me," Liam answered. In that moment, his uncle's question slapped like a ball against a wall and bounced back at him. The words were in Liam's head a second time—*that Mr. Hapwood paid you . . . How did Uncle Patrick know*?

"It was Mr. Gavin who saw you late this afternoon in that cart of Mr. Hapwood's, returning from wherever you two had gone," Uncle Patrick said. "Alice Ann told me of the rest."

"And where is she?"

"Oh, she has run off to her Mrs. McCathery. No wish had she to be here when you came home."

Caught in Uncle Patrick's glare, Liam's breath stopped. He waited for his uncle to bolt at him in fury, like Dudley had when chasing Colin. Liam edged closer to the door. Uncle Patrick was folding his paper into neat squares. "Bring me the strap," he said in a cold voice.

When Liam did not move, his voice sharpened. "Bring it! Sure you know you deserve the strap for disobeying me. From the first, I said you were not to work for that man."

He could run, Liam told himself. He could be out the door in a moment. But his feet didn't move. "You told me I couldn't," he said to Uncle Patrick. "I know you did."

Keep going forward, Jacob had said.

Liam took three steps toward his uncle and sat across from him. His uncle's face was tight with rage. "Hear me out," Liam pleaded.

"You did a thing I told you not to do. There is little to hear beyond that."

Liam said, "One day a man came into Mr. O'Donnell's shop. He looked like Father. I followed him to see if he was. That's why Mr. O'Donnell fired me, because I left. And that's why I asked Mr. Hapwood to hire me—so you would have your money."

Uncle Patrick rapped a drumbeat on the table with his knuckles, his lips pressed tightly together. Liam said, "I had to find out if the man was my father."

"He is not worth the finding, that father of yours."

"You said yourself that his blood runs in my veins."

Uncle Patrick spit out words. "His blood—that is a fact!"

"But Mum's blood, too. It's Mum who sent us here," Liam argued, "and I thought it might have been so I could find him."

"Your mother?" Uncle Patrick ran a finger across his thin mustache. Back and forth it went. "Molly was dead when Mrs. McCathery's letter came to my cabin. She had nothing to do with your coming here. Have your brains gone muddled?"

"Before Mum died, she wrote to Mrs. McCathery. Mum asked her to write you, to make you come here. She wanted you to bring us."

His uncle shook his head, denying it.

"Ask Mrs. McCathery if you don't believe me," Liam insisted. "Mum wanted you to bring us here because she was afraid of you."

"Afraid? Wasn't I both brother and father to her—our parents dead, when she was only nine, the cart tumbling off the road and them with it, God have mercy on their souls. Through the years, it was myself that raised her. Never did Molly fear me. Everywhere I went, when she was a little girl, she would beg to follow along."

"When Mum knew she would die, she was afraid, afraid for us—and hasn't Alice Ann run off to Mrs. McCathery because she's terrified of what you'll do to me?"

Uncle Patrick stared at him. "What I'll do? And where is the strap I told you to bring then?"

Liam leaned away from him, pressing his back against the back of the chair. He wouldn't fetch the strap. He wouldn't play a part any longer. He said, "Mum wanted us to come here. She wanted us to meet Mrs.

McCathery. She wanted us to see this world, so we could decide whether to go back to Connemara or stay."

"Stay? And you working for that black man?" Uncle Patrick frowned.

"Uncle, please, I only want—"

"I will look for land through the winter," Uncle Patrick insisted. "I'll plant my own land in the spring, not another man's this time! And you'll work by me. In the end you'll know what work means, boyo. I'll turn you into an Irishman yet." He tilted his chair back, stared up at the ceiling, and said, "If I look at your sister, I see Molly, but I see no trace of your mother in you, boyo." Uncle Patrick's chair banged back down. He looked at Liam and repeated the claim—"There's not a trace of Molly in you."

Liam replied angrily, "Aren't I speaking Gaelic now because Mum spoke it with us? Don't I remember everything she did and everything she said? She's my mother, too."

His uncle made a steeple of his hands. He leaned his forehead against it and shut his eyes.

"And wasn't I with her when she was dying?" Liam asked.

He remembered how the cook had fetched him that night from the basement room that he shared with the assistant gardener. At her side, he had mounted to the women's quarters in the attic, where normally no man or boy could go. It was night. Gas lamps lit their way. Liam had counted the steps as they climbed from floor to floor. There were eighty-nine of them.

Alice Ann was in the room when he arrived, sitting on a stool. He perched on its edge, next to her. Mum watched the two of them, smiling once. She closed her eyes after that—because things looked too bright, she told them, the candles by her bed that had burnt down by half, and even their faces.

"Mum didn't want Lord Clapham ordering us about. She made sure we would leave there after she died," Liam said to his uncle. "She wanted no one to order us about."

Uncle Patrick's eyes were still closed. On his steepled hands the tendons made ridges. If he turned them over, Liam knew he would see calluses on the palms that marked a life of hard work. And Uncle Patrick had little to show for that work, Liam admitted. There he was, sitting on a shabby chair in front of a table that wobbled.

"Uncle?"

The flame in the kerosene light wavered. Uncle Patrick watched it. He didn't look at Liam. "No, she would not want you staying with Lord Clapham. Of course, Molly wouldn't," he said. "Wasn't it a Lord Clapham who asked for armed guards in famine times. Needed guards the fine gentry did, God knows, taking the wheat and corn and cattle off to the ports while people were dying for want of a mere morsel."

In his distant monotone, Uncle Patrick could be leading a séance—bringing the dead to the table to have their say. He had lost Uncle Patrick to this spell, Liam realized. There was nothing more to say to him. But there would be no strap either.

In their room, Liam took the long shirt he slept in from the basket where he kept his things. He put it on and lay down on his mattress, back against the wall.

He dozed. He woke. His uncle had climbed onto the rickety bedstead, only a few feet away. He was wrapping himself in his quilt. After a few minutes, Liam heard the steady shuffling of his breath, which meant he was asleep. Would he dream tonight of fighting against the English? Liam suddenly felt sad. It was that his uncle chose to fight his battles and did not choose at all. He was caught in history's snare. He was trapped.

Battles—Liam thought of the chicken's head in his mouth and of Colin's fractured bone, slick with blood, under his fingers, and of how Dudley's legs had buckled under him when Mr. Hapwood fired the gun. He wanted no more of battle.

Eight days after they put Dudley down, Colin came home from the hospital. Liam saw him through the open door of his apartment, lying on a bed they had moved to the front room. He wore a grim expression, but he had both legs because the surgeons at the hospital had decided not to amputate the injured one.

The next day, Liam carried up a tureen of fish soup that Mrs. McCathery had made. "I would take it up myself," she said to him, "but I have an appointment with one of my fine ladies. Mrs. Fisher does not abide anyone's being late. Always in a fluster she is, over something or another, her gowns, of course, or the state of her constitution—her lungs and her pulsations." She shook her head. "Now take the soup up to Mr. Gavin. There's a good lad." She gave Liam a kind look.

Two minutes later, in Mr. Gavin's kitchen, Mr. Gavin was dishing it out. He handed the bowl and a spoon to Liam. "Give that to Colin."

Liam carried the soup to the front room, where Colin sat in his bed, crutches across his lap. "My father told me that Mr. Hapwood shot Dudley," Colin said as he put his crutches aside and took the soup and the spoon from Liam.

"Mrs. McCathery thought the horse might kill somebody yet," Liam replied. "Uncle Patrick and your father wanted him dead, too, so we put the horse down, Mr. Hapwood and me."

"That horse deserved a bullet."

"But if we hadn't gone near him, if we had—"

Colin interrupted. "Or if you had stayed on his back."

"You ordered me to ride him. You had a part in it."

"Ordered you, I did." Colin stirred the soup. Against the side of the bowl, his spoon made a clicking noise. "I have always been under orders concerning you. Long ago I told you of my orders."

Liam said, "They were Michael Lanigan's orders, but he's far away. Why do you want to fight with me here?"

Colin spooned out a piece of cod and ate it. "If Ireland is going to be free, men must fight for her."

"But our own fight was senseless from the start."

"I followed Michael Lanigan's orders then. I follow them now."

"So, does he own you?" It was the same furious question Mr. Hapwood had asked only nine nights ago — *You doin' just exactly what he says, like that boy owns you?* Colin didn't answer it. He only stared at Liam, who said, "Didn't I pull Dudley off you? You'd be dead if I hadn't."

Colin glowered at Liam but said nothing because his father came into the room. Liam didn't care if Colin glowered. When he had run for help, to rescue Colin, the wind had made an eerie noise, rushing through the trees. It had sounded like an accusing voice. If Colin had died, that voice would pursue him still. It would haunt him forever. Colin *would* own him, in fact.

But he had fought the horse for Colin's life. He had not let Colin die, and so it was finished. He was free.

CHAPTER SEVENTEEN

THREE WEEKS WENT BY. It was mid-May. Just as April had been unseasonably cold with its snows, May was unseasonably hot. The temperature went higher and higher during the day. By night, the small apartments were as hot as ovens.

People took to sleeping on the roof, carrying up bedding. Mr. Gavin asked Liam to help him lug Colin's mattress to the roof. "Without it, he will be in so much pain that he won't be able to sleep," Mr. Gavin said.

They carried the mattress out of Mr. Gavin's rooms. From the bottom of the stairs, Colin watched them struggle up the first three steps. Then, as they reached the fourth, he thumped toward them on one crutch, tossing the other aside. He grabbed at a corner of the mattress and shouldered it. "Don't," he said to Mr. Gavin, when his father tried to take the weight from him. "I can do it."

When Colin looked at Liam, there was no hatred in

his eyes, only pain. Colin took one more step up and then another. He could never like Colin, Liam decided, but he wanted him to make it up these stairs.

An hour later, people were settling into place. Jacob was beside Liam, talking of electrons running along a wire to light a bulb and of how a million of them would fit on the head of pin. As always, his voice grew more excited the more he talked. He might work with electricity, he said, if he became a scientist. "There is a scholarship I am going to try for, the Pulitzer scholarship for Columbia University. I'd study there, if I get it." In a moment, with the same enthusiasm, he said, "I'm going to a baseball game in Washington Heights in a few days. I'll take you with me. I'll teach you about baseball."

"At the end of September, when my uncle leaves, he wants to take me with him," Liam told him.

Jacob said something else. Then Liam spoke. Back and forth their voices went, while Liam watched the stars, which filled the wide, dark sky. Linked, they formed constellations. Jacob yawned. As if answering, Liam yawned, too. He was thinking that on this roof people made human constellations, gathering with those they claimed as their own. Jacob lay near him, sliding into sleep. On Jacob's other side, his family had put down bedding an hour ago. Mrs. McCathery had settled next to Alice Ann and Uncle Patrick. Her two boarders stayed together near the roof's edge with three other workingmen.

Constellations—Liam made one of his own, choosing a star directly over his head for his mother. From those that surrounded it, he assigned stars to Alice Ann, Mrs. McCathery, Mr. Hapwood, Jacob, and himself. He memorized their positions so he could find the formation again.

He did not give a star to his father because he had married Mum, lying to her and disgracing her. He did not deserve a star. He might never see his father again. Liam did not know if he even wanted to.

But that same night Liam dreamed of him. In the dream, Liam was riding a horse. At first, he seemed to be Delmonico, but then the animal's coat changed color. All at once, Liam was up on Morengo, Lord Clapham's stallion, with his white and brown markings. He and the horse flew past a scarecrow with a battered hat and stick arms, like the one in Mr. Hapwood's garden. The scarecrow had come alive and was hurling dented buckets in every direction. One hit Morengo, who took fright. Wild-eyed, he galloped faster, so fast that the landscape blurred, so fast that the reins were torn out of Liam's hands. Every time he reached for them, they slipped away. Beneath Liam, thudding hooves turned up dirt and stones. He was sure that the hooves would crush him if he tumbled off the horse's back. Someone called to him. The voice urged him to lean forward and dig his heels in and hold tight to the horse's mane and center his weight. It was his father's voice. He bent over the horse. He tried with all his might to do what he was told, but he started to slide off, losing his balance.

Liam woke with a jagged cry, fists clenched and knees drawn up toward his chest, as if he were riding. His heart beat at a gallop, and he was still listening with all his might for his father's voice.

Jacob made a grumbling noise and turned over. His eyes opened. "What is it?"

"It was a dream," Liam said as he stared at the stars. His father seemed to be as far away as they were. His father would never rescue him.

Liam sat up, his arms around his knees. He thought of riding Morengo through the woods to meet the boys at the stream. He had done that without his father's help, and he hadn't fallen off the horse, though he was only a child of nine. If he rode Morengo now, he wouldn't fall off.

And, without his father's help, he could remain in this city, too. "I won't go back to Ireland," he told Jacob. "I'm staying in New York. It's what I want."

"What about your uncle?"

"He doesn't own me. He won't kidnap me and drag me onto the boat. Mrs. McCathery will help me if I tell her I want to stay here. I'm sure of it. That's two of us against him."

"Make it three," Jacob said, grinning. "I'm on your side."

Liam lay back down. He was a boy from Ireland, but he belonged here now. He studied the stars in the American sky above him. Uncle Patrick would go back and buy his land because he belonged in Ireland, and Ireland had a sky, too. In it, his uncle's star would burn furiously in coming years. Mr. Gavin's star would be right next to Uncle Patrick's star, and Colin's star would be by Mr. Gavin's. In a fierce constellation, hundreds of stars would cluster together in that Irish sky, as close as men in battle.

When he rolled over, Liam saw that Jacob was asleep again. He could see the rise and fall of breath in his chest. If he made a new life in this new world, like Jacob was doing, he had to make it out of things that were real, not of out of fantasies of what might be, and not out of dreams of his father. Like Jacob, he'd shape a life from real things that he could reach and touch.

The weather grew hotter still. Every day Liam went off with Mr. Hapwood. Flies buzzed and bit, and Delmonico flicked his ears to drive them off. The hot winds carried dust made of dirt, manure, and grit. Sometimes, fending the dust off, Mr. Hapwood drew a kerchief up over his nose like a cowboy.

People would wave to the wagon. Mr. Hapwood waved back. Sometimes when they called to him, Mr. Hapwood would pull to the side of the street, and there would be a slow, polite conversation about a cousin's health or a church meeting. There would be a joke, and Mr. Hapwood's laughter. For all the talk with everyone else, Mr. Hapwood was often silent when he rode with Liam, especially in the weeks after Dudley was put down, but gradually the silence broke, like ice breaking in a thaw. One day, out of the blue, Mr. Hapwood suddenly said, "Don't worry none about not pulling that trigger on Dudley, 'bout not *wanting* to shoot a horse in the head. You hear me?"

On another day, sitting on the wagon's bench as Delmonico pulled them along, Liam found himself telling Mr. Hapwood about things his grandmother had witnessed in famine times. He told him of how his grandmother had seen a woman and a child sneak into a stable yard behind an inn one night. A horse was tethered there. The woman made a small cut in its neck with a razor and held a tin cup below it to catch its blood. She put the cup to her child's mouth, urging him to sip, not wanting him to starve.

Another day, Liam told Mr. Hapwood a thing Mrs. McCathery had told him—that the English had sent Irish people into slavery. Mr. Hapwood looked at him suspiciously. Liam said, "Oliver Cromwell was England's master then, and he invaded Ireland. People who didn't leave their own land for poor land in the west of Ireland, like Cromwell ordered, why they were slaughtered or sent off to the West Indies. They made slaves of them there."

"First I knew anything of that," Mr. Hapwood said. Liam sensed he still did not believe it was true.

The wagon came to a stop in front of a church. Liam climbed into its bed and began wrestling with an organ they were to deliver. "Hop down now," Mr. Hapwood said. Liam did. He caught his end when Mr. Hapwood shoved the organ off the wagon's edge. "You got this dang thing steady?" Mr. Hapwood asked. "Watch out for that pothole there by your right foot or you're gonna trip."

Liam became accustomed to Mr. Hapwood's gruff orders or to warnings like this one, meant to save his skin.

June passed quickly. At the end of the month, on Saint

Peter's Day, Mrs. McCathery and Uncle Patrick, Liam and Alice Ann, and Colin and his father went to Mass at Sacred Heart Church, not far from where they lived. They sat together on the pew. They knelt together. They took communion, passing up the aisle in a line.

Afterward, outside the church, people gathered in small groups. Many spoke with a thick Irish brogue; others spoke in Gaelic. Mrs. McCathery talked with a woman whose daughter had applied for job as a maid. "Rose was told straight to her face that an Irish girl might baptize children when no one was looking and make them into little Catholics," she complained. "They wouldn't hire Rose, or any Irish girl."

Mrs. McCathery made a face. "Stuff and nonsense!"

A man tapped the woman's arm. "Why, they are hiring girls at Child's, the restaurant. Hannah's cousin Elsie was hired only yesterday. She might put in a good word for Rose there."

Mrs. McCathery winked at Uncle Patrick. "We are like a tribe of Indians here, only Irish, every last one of us. We are an Irish tribe, and don't we take care of each other just fine?"

When Liam woke in the middle of that same night, a candle was burning. His uncle hovered over it, hands clasped in front of him, the light shining on his lined face.

"Uncle, are you sick?"

Uncle Patrick shook his head. "No." He wiped sweat from his forehead. His skin was flushed and his face fearful. "Your mother, when she was two years old or three, she might beg and beg for a half-penny's worth of candy. Sure you'd think her heart was breaking straight in half. If she couldn't have what she wanted, she'd turn into a half-wild little thing."

Liam drew the blanket up over his shoulders. The candlelight flickered on the ceiling. Grimacing, Uncle Patrick blew the candle out. The room was suddenly dark. "Go back to sleep," he commanded. Liam couldn't see Uncle Patrick any longer and didn't know if he slept again because he fell asleep himself.

The next morning Uncle Patrick didn't look as if he had slept. He seemed worn-out. He held a cap in his hands and fiddled with its brim. "You are not afraid of work," he said to Liam. "I'll not deny that. Sometimes you are out that door before I am myself." His voice was so low he could be talking to himself.

Liam spread butter on a slice of bread. "No, I am not afraid of work," he said.

"Almost a man you are."

Liam looked at him. He had never heard words like this come out of Uncle Patrick's mouth.

"In the end, I am after thinking, it will do no good to make you go back to Ireland when I go, if you want no part of it," Uncle Patrick said. "If you want, stay here." He turned the cap in his hands. It went around and around. His head jerked up. He looked straight at Liam. "From time to time I dream of Molly. Last night she was begging me to let you have your way. She was wild-eyed. She said she'd never come again if I didn't do what she asked. I would lose her for good."

Uncle Patrick moved to the door. He left swiftly, slamming it behind him. He left before Liam could thank him.

Another Sunday came. An Irish fair was taking place at Celtic Park in Queens. "You should come, Liam. Mr. Gavin invited you, too," Alice Ann said. She drew a tortoise shell comb through her hair.

Liam shook his head. "I'm going to look at some horses with Mr. Hapwood. The riding stable is selling some, and he's thinking of buying one."

She made a face at him. When Alice Ann came home, she made the same face and declared, "Liam, you should have come, like I told you to."

"I should have," he answered. "Mr. Hapwood never did find a horse he liked."

"There was a shooting range. They had foot races and hurling," Alice Ann said. Sitting on chair, Uncle Patrick polished his shoes with a rag, looking from the shoe in his hand to Alice Ann, taking note of what she said.

"And there was music. I danced with a dozen boys, until I couldn't dance anymore." Alice Ann bent down and took off her shoes. She wiggled her toes.

Uncle Patrick watched her. He said, "Your mother, how she loved a dance. You should have seen Molly then, whirling around and around. Her skirts would go flying. Her hair would fly."

Uncle Patrick stared into space. Liam thought that he was seeing Mum, the way he himself could sometimes see her—as if she were alive again.

Alice Ann broke the silence. "It was like a fair in

Ireland itself, the man with magic tricks and the fortune-tellers, and meat pies and stewed apples. There was—"

Uncle Patrick broke in. "You stay, too, if you want. Stay with Liam and with Mrs. McCathery and with the Irish tribe she's so proud of. I won't drag you away either!"

Abruptly, he slipped on his shoes and stood. He put the rag and polish away. He pulled on the shirt that Alice Ann had washed and ironed the day before. Alice Ann stepped forward. She reached out and started to button it for him. Uncle Patrick startled, like a green, untrained horse might if someone touched it. Backing away, buttoning the shirt himself, he left.

As soon as he was out the door, Alice Ann said, "I never thought he would tell me I could stay here."

"It was Mum who made him say that," Liam said. "Mum in a dream he had. Mum dancing in front of his eyes just now."

"So I can stay if I want," Alice Ann murmured. "But I think of Ireland every single day." She smoothed her skirt. "I think of the green hills and the sea. There is nothing like that here. Nothing at all."

Liam remembered all that Alice Ann did. He remembered the horses in the meadows, too, and how the smell of grass filled the air. He remembered fishing a favorite stream, the clear, cold water rushing against his legs. He missed all that. But he remembered other things, things he did not miss. "Lady Clapham thought she owned Mum, the way she treated her sometimes," he said.

Alice Ann sat down on the chair where Uncle Patrick had just sat. She stared straight ahead, brow furrowed.

Liam said, "The Irish will fight the English, wanting Ireland back. The fighting will go on and on. "

Alice Ann didn't move. She didn't even blink. Liam said, "There, we'd be trapped. Here, we could start over."

He was pleading, Liam realized. His sister was all he had of family now. He wanted her to stay. But if she wanted to return to Ireland, he couldn't stop her. He shouldn't even try. No one should. He said nothing more.

Her brow still furrowed in thought, Alice Ann stood again. She faced Liam, hands clasped in front of her, silent. Then she wet her lips with her tongue and words rushed out of her mouth. "Mrs. McCathery would help us. And you and me, we could make something of this place if we tried. There's paint. It costs nothing." She looked at the windows. "I could hang curtains." Eagerly, she looked back at Liam. "We'd be starting over, like you said. It will be a brand new life. Mum would want that."

Liam took the blue-gray stone from his pocket. He held it out to his sister. "What is it?" she asked, taking it.

"I found it by Mum's grave. It's Mum's stone."

The stone lay on the palm of her right hand. "She'll never leave us," Alice Ann said softly, before returning the stone to Liam. She watched him slip it back into his pocket. "We'll stay. Mum will be with us."

With a pitchfork, Mr. Hapwood tossed hay into a manger. "Tomorrow I'm gonna look at some more horses," he said to Liam. "You come with me again. A man got a string of them he bought from another fella in Kentucky."

The next day, they traveled in the wagon to a breeding

farm located north of the city. There were ramshackle buildings and horses grazing in fields.

Mr. Hapwood fed and watered Delmonico and tied him to a tree. "Now let's go see what's here," he said.

Liam followed Mr. Hapwood to a paddock, where a dozen yearlings ambled about. Mr. Hapwood stood in front of one—a chestnut filly with a star and white stockings. "This one, no wonder he wants to be rid of her." He ran his cupped hands down a rear leg. "Capped hock, these lumpy fetlocks," he said. "That tail of hers, stuck on her low down. She is one sorry sight."

Liam looked around him. Horses were everywhere, near and far. Beyond the dozen paddocks and the stables, a white fence ran along one side of a slanting hill. A rider descended the hill, a woman riding sidesaddle, a red riding cap on her head. "Go look around," Mr. Hapwood said, seeing his interest. "I got inspecting to do myself. We're gonna find each other in a little bit."

He wandered one way, Liam another.

It was Liam who first noticed the black colt. He had a single white streak down his chest. To the side of the streak were splatters. It looked as if somebody had loaded a brush with paint and applied it carelessly to his coat.

When Liam approached, the colt took a step toward him. Mr. Hapwood came up behind Liam. "You like the looks of that one?"

The colt was shoving his nose toward them, curious or looking for a handout. "He's put together right, I'll say that, the way he sits solid on all four legs. And he's got some power in those hindquarters," Mr. Hapwood said.

Liam ran a hand along the colt's arched neck.

"Hold his head." Mr. Hapwood crouched down, feeling the colt's knees and fetlock joints, pinching at ligaments and tendons. He stood again, prying the colt's mouth open. "Still got his milk teeth. He won't get any permanent teeth 'til he's about three."

He ordered Liam to stay by the animal. Twenty-five minutes later, when he returned, Mr. Hapwood said the colt's papers showed a stallion two generations back that had raced hard. "A long string of foals came out of him. Some of them raced strong. Not all of them, that's the thing. And this one, the knees are splayed some, see that? He's a mite short. Course we don't got the money for any horse that's a sure bet, that everybody wants. One way or the other, it's gonna be a gamble."

Again Mr. Hapwood inspected the colt, talking to Liam about everything he found and why it counted for the colt or against the colt. He told Liam to grab onto his halter and lead him through his paces.

"His foreleg goes swinging out some," Mr. Hapwood mused when he and Liam stood side by side once again, the colt in front of them. "But his gait's smooth. And those splayed knees of his don't seem to bother him when he gets to travelin'."

Mr. Hapwood clasped his hands together in front of him, almost as if he were praying. In a moment, his hands went into his pockets and he said, "We're gonna go for it."

The two of them stood in the office in front of the owner, who tilted his desk chair backward and forward. Standing near was another man, dressed in checkered trousers and a tweed cap, who said he'd buy three horses, including the colt. Mr. Hapwood offered the asking price of two hundred and fifty dollars. The other man offered two hundred and seventy-five while he peered at Mr. Hapwood through bloodshot eyes.

Only that morning Mr. Hapwood had told Liam that he had three hundred dollars, and that was the end of it. Now he said he would pay that much.

The man could not know that was all that was in Mr. Hapwood's pocket, Liam told himself. He could have no idea how high Mr. Hapwood could bid.

The colt's owner pointed the lit end of his cigar at the man in the checkered trousers. "Three hundred dollars, this fella just said. You heard him. So what do you say to that?"

"Those knobby knees, and the horse isn't that big either," the man answered. "I'm not going any higher. He can have that animal if he wants it so bad."

The colt's owner puffed on the cigar and rocked back on his chair. His voice rose over the chair's loud creaking. "Mr. Hapwood, you got yourself a deal! You got yourself a nice little colt for that amount of money."

"Half of these are Mrs. McCathery's," Mr. Hapwood told Liam, slapping bills down, one by one, on the desk while the owner counted them. "We owned Dudley together. We'll own this horse together."

Outside, Liam tied the colt to the wagon. The colt followed them home willingly, it seemed, like a puppy might follow along. Now and again Mr. Hapwood would look back at him. Twice they stopped to give the colt and Delmonico water.

Home again, in the stable, Liam watched Mr. Hapwood rub the colt down with a sack. He would at times stretch his arms across the colt's back and lean over. "Get him used to some weight on his back, and the feel and the smell of me, too. Do it right off," he said.

When Liam brought the colt a bucket of water, Mr. Hapwood said, "Tomorrow we'll get him out in the yard, start him in on his lessons — fifteen minutes, twenty minutes at a time, two or three times a day. That's what you do if you want to keep a horse interested. Don't want to bore him." He paused. "You like horses like you seem to do, it's about time you learned how to train one."

"Yes, sir," Liam said. In that moment he saw how he would come into the stable every morning, arriving even before Mr. Hapwood did. He would muck out the colt's stall and lay down fresh straw. He would scour out the colt's bucket, bring him feed and water, curry his coat, and inspect his hooves. He would take him outside and exercise him in the yard.

Mr. Hapwood said, "We give him hay to take the edge off his appetite before we give him oats." He laid a warning eye on Liam. "You know you never give a horse his fill of oats?"

"Oats are too rich," Liam replied. "Oats might give a horse colic, especially if he drinks right away and they swell up in his stomach."

Mr. Hapwood nodded. "You know what you know, but you're gonna know a lot more before we're finished with him." After a few seconds he added, "So this about does it."

It was all he said, but Liam guessed at what Mr.

Hapwood meant—that the black colt was here now and that, more and more, Dudley would be a memory, part of a past. The past counted, and Dudley's death counted, but the past was not an inescapable jail cell. He and Mr. Hapwood were not locked up in the past forever and ever. There was a future, and they were free to search that future out.

Tomorrow they might give the colt a name. Soon he would know commands and take a saddle and a bit and, before long, a rider. One day, he would race. This colt would be a different animal by then, fully-grown and sure of himself, his neck stretched forward, taking long, hard strides. On that day, Liam hoped, he would be on the colt's back.

There was a past and a future, and there was a present, too. In it, Mr. Hapwood was offering the black colt a handful of hay. Light fell from the window above the stall door and splashed across the colt's coat. Liam put his hand out and stroked his neck. The colt was something he could reach and touch. You made a life out of things you could touch. The colt lifted his head and, eyes wide, looked straight at him.

Author's Note

My novel traces Ireland's moving history, most particularly, her centuries-long conflict with England. It also describes the lives of the Irish and the African-Americans who lived side by side in Hell's Kitchen at the turn of the last century. There are records of good relationships between these groups during this era, and even inter-marriages. Dreadful conflicts are also recorded, including the race riot Mr. Hapwood so vividly describes.

Through extensive research and on-site exploration in Connemara, Ireland, and in New York City, I have tried to ensure that *A Boy from Ireland*, though fiction, accurately portrays these historical realities. Fiction, I believe, should steer readers toward truth, not mislead them.

The many background details supplied in *A Boy from Ireland* are true, as well. In Ireland, for example, there were tough, robust Connemara ponies. The United States stamp on Uncle Patrick's letter would have pictured Benjamin Franklin. Dudley Allen was the black owner and trainer of a horse that won the Kentucky Derby, and an Irish politician by the name of George Washington Plunkitt ran affairs in Hell's Kitchen. Illegal cockfights did take place, a rider did announce the coming of a train on the hazardous Eleventh Avenue tracks, and a small replica of the Statue of Liberty topped a building called the Liberty Warehouse.

I apologize for any inaccuracies that may appear in the novel in spite of my careful research, but one is deliberate. In 1901, African-Americans would have referred to themselves—with pride—as *Negroes* or as *colored*. (The National Association for the Advancement of Colored People was founded in 1909.) Times change, however, as do people's inclinations. Should I have used the historically accurate terms *Negro* or *colored* instead of the term *black*? Should I have respected the wishes of the people of yesterday or the wishes of the people of today? Readers may want to debate this question.

About the Author

 Marie Raphael is a life-long educator who has worked with young people at many levels and in many situations — from a Harlem preschool in New York City to college classrooms in Boston and California to a rural junior high school. Most recently, she supervised student teachers at Humboldt State University in California. She is the author of two immigrant adventure novels, *Streets of Gold* and *A Boy from Ireland*. She lives with her husband in northern California.